John Hutchinson Garnier

Prince Pedro

A Tragedy

John Hutchinson Garnier

Prince Pedro
A Tragedy

ISBN/EAN: 9783744749534

Printed in Europe, USA, Canada, Australia, Japan

Cover: Foto ©Andreas Hilbeck / pixelio.de

More available books at **www.hansebooks.com**

PRINCE PEDRO:

A TRAGEDY.

BY

J. H. GARNIER, M.D.

TORONTO :
BELFORD BROTHERS.
1877.

HUNTER, ROSE & CO.,
PRINTERS AND BINDERS
TORONTO.

Dedication.

—

MAY IT PLEASE YOUR EXCELLENCY,

Allow me with every feeling of respect, to inscribe the following play to your Lordship.

It is my first attempt, and although, doubtless, inferior to productions of more gifted authors, yet if it give you any pleasure in its perusal, I shall be content. Yourself, a man of letters, can easily understand the anxiety of an author when casting the first effusions of his muse on the ocean of literature. If "Prince Pedro," meet with your honest approval on its own merits, as a dramatic production, I shall have little to fear from the asperities of critics. I cannot sufficiently express my thanks for the kindness you have extended to me, in permitting me to dedicate this tragedy to Your Excellency; and I really feel it to be no small favor and honor.

Allow me to subscribe myself,

Your Excellency's

Most obedient,

JOHN H. GARNIER, M. D,

Lucknow, Ont.,
February 19th, 1877,

Dramatis Personæ.

MALES.

PEDRO, Prince of Portugal.

ALFONSO, King of Portugal.

RUDOLPHO, } Noblemen.
PECHICO,

LUDRO, Abbot of Cintra.

MATTEO DE CASTRO, a noble, brother of Inez.

SEBASTIAN, } Servants
RODRIGO, { of
ALONZO, { Matteo.
MARCO,

SANCHO, } Retainer of Ludro,
LORENZO, } Pechico's hired assassin.

SUAREZ, a noble.

RAYMOND, Ambassador of Navarre,

CARLOS, } Children of
ALFONSO, } Pedro.

A Troubadour, Guards, &c., Beggar.

A Judge.

FEMALES.

QUEEN OF PORTUGAL.

INEZ DE CASTRO, wife of Pedro.

PAULINE, wife of Pechico.

ISABELLA, daughter of Rudolpho, companion of Inez.

XARA, Servant and Moorish attendant of Inez.

Ladies in waiting, &c.

PRINCE PEDRO.

ACT I.

SCENE I.—A HALL IN MATTEO'S CASTLE.

LUDRO, MATTEO, RODRIGO (*conversing*).

MATTEO.

I TELL thee, abbot, that I want mine own.
Who held mine uncle's hand to sign this deed?
My mother's broad estate, must I lose that!
I tell thee, that before I left his couch—
Before the breath had parted from his lips,
His lips, and teeth, and mouth, and tongue and
    throat,—
Gave all the earthly goods he had to me.
My uncle and my sire both made me pledge
My honor as a noble of Castile,
That I should sink the crescent 'neath the cross.
How then can come this will? Who wrote it
    down?
Who ever heard of it except thyself?

LUDRO.

If this will had not been, whence doth it come?
That will bequeathes, in thy good uncle's name,
All things to Cintra. What mean you, my lord,
To call this will a forgery? Who forged
This instrument? (*Holds up the parchment.*)

MATTEO.

Now hearken, noble sir. Was I not born
To heir mine own estates, left to me by
My sire,—*my* mother—and mine uncle,—who—
But yesterday, and when the breath was thick,
And struggling in his breast for mastery,
Bequeathed me all he had. I never left
His presence till he died. His head was laid
Tenderly on my breast, and his last sigh
Sped up to heaven, as I held his form
Clasped in mine arms. See you lie not to me.—
I tell thee that thyself hast framed the will;
And could the parchment speak, 'twould loudly say:
Vile monk, this deed I am, is forged by thee.
Is Inez likewise to be robbed of all?
Are we to be vile outcasts? Give me that will,—
For forgery is writ upon thy face!

LUDRO.

I prithee, my most noble count, beware!
This instrument is in just form, and true;

Witnessed, and sealed, and given unto me.
I claim this gift of your good uncle, dead,—
See, then, my lord, 'tis mine.   I have this bond,
And by this bond my tenure stands or falls.
'Tis most precise in each particular.
I've read it over, with much pains, to learn
If aught might prove amiss, and 'tis correct,
Aye, most correct and unimpeachable.
Nay, then, my lord, if thou art so inclined,
Go, test thy claim at law.

MATTEO.

So be it, for the mummery thou actest,
Will yet return, like viper, to thy breast,
And sting thee to the quick, poor lying knave !
But listen, Ludro, though thou art a monk,
And cozen all, thou shalt not cozen me.——
Mine own shall be mine own !   Give me mine own.
What ! would'st thou rob my sister and myself,
By thy false instrument, so basely forged ?
How comes it I ne'er knew such claim before ;
And why did not mine uncle ere he died,
Give me some mention of it !

LUDRO.

Seek the law,
And thou wilt get all justice there; my lord.
Nay, call me as thou wilt, words are but words.

But see, I hold this parchment in my hand;
And holding it, I hold thy lands: and know——
That I will hold them.   [*Exit.*

MATTEO.

And can it be, Rodrigo, that this man
Hath any reason, or a conscience left,
To show such villainy in such a claim!
He's gone; and as he went, I marked the frown
That nestled on his brow! There's mischief there.
A snake most venomous twined in his brain.
Methought, I saw its eyes glitter from out
His eyes, so full of hate and deathliness.
I grieve not for myself. I am a man;
And I can fight mankind, and win my way.
But my poor sister, what is she to do?
Can she forego her home;—can she endure
To see our lands, and all that we possess,
Claimed by these monks? Full well I know and
    feel
That if the world doth pity as you pass,
And smile in sympathy—that sympathy
Bears to the heart full many a mortal ill;
'Tis like December's sun, cold, drear, and chill!

RODRIGO.

Most worthy master, be not so cast down.
Ludro asks for the law, which shall explain

The mystery of this will.   Pechico, sir,
Declares himself your friend.   Methinks his heart
Clings to the Lady Inez lovingly.
Then be not so down-hearted, till just cause
Appears more real, than the vapoury noise
Of this defiant monk.   Justice is yours,
And I have heard it said, Justice and Truth
Are twins immortal, man can never part.
Then trust in Justice, and her sister, Truth !

MATTEO.

The law is but the law, and never sure.

RODRIGO.

But truth and justice always must endure.
                                   [*Exeunt.*

SCENE II.—A HALL IN THE PALACE IN LISBON.

PRINCE PEDRO, PECHICO, RUDOLPHO—*Attendants,
     equipped for the Journey.*

RUDOLPHO.

Most gracious Prince ! what am I now to do ?
I gave all orders for the chase.   Our horses

Are here ready.   The dogs are in the leash.
The hawks all hooded, and the men are busy,
As such rascals always are,—doing,—nothing !
When may it please the Prince to start ?

PEDRO.

I got a letter even now from Spain,
From our old friend, the Count of Aguilar,
Who asks that I do spend a season there,
And promises the very best of sport.
He says, bears are in plenty ; and the deer,
And every thing besides, as one could wish.
Wolves very numerous, and herons too ;
And winged game, for those who love to hawk.
What say you, gentlemen, if we go there,
And do forego the pleasures of to-day.
I do so love to hunt the savage bear,
And see the wolf all bloody at my feet.
What say you if we visit Aguilar ;
We'll have rare sport no doubt.

RUDOLPHO.

                             As it may please
Yourself, it pleases me.   There are good streams
Amidst those rocky hills, where scaly victims swim;
I love to angle, better than the chase.
It is more gentle sport.

PECHICO.

                              Perchance it be—
But I am like the Prince, delighting more
To hear the winding horn echo from rock
To rock.   To see the stealthy wolf come forth,
Creeping along, and, with a furtive glance,
Look careful back, to note where comes the hound.
Then as he higher rises to my view,
I love to let the whistling arrow sing,
And pierce the cottage robber to the heart.
Almost I think I see his glazing eye ;
Almost I hear his dismal dying growl ;
Half stifled, gurgling in his hollow throat ;
And see the bloody froth come bubbling forth.
Then, as he snarls and shows his crimsoned fangs,
I see that savage grin,—the grin of death.
What do you think, Prince Pedro, of my tale ?
Is such not manlier sport than wandering,
Like Rudolpho with a basket in his hand ;
Pulling forth kicking fishes from the brook,
Dangling upon his rod.—Oh, ha ! ha ! ha !

PEDRO.

My Lord Pechico, be not so severe, ·
For all men love not woodland sports alike ;
I love to chase the bear, or deer, or wolf,
As does yourself.   Another loves his hawk,

Another loves his war horse as his life.
Some love to course the hare, and some to angle.

RUDOLPHO.

Nay let him laugh, Prince Pedro, let him laugh.
I'll take my kicking fishes for my sport,
Dangling upon my hook.   Then as I come—
Most hungry from the brook, I love to feed
On fishes broiled, not eat a stinking wolf.
Pechico, some broiled wolf.   Oh, ha ! ha ! ha !
(*All laugh.*)

Enter KING ALFONSO *and attendants.*

ALFONSO.

My lords, you seem in merry mood to-day !
The Prince takes ample pleasure in the woods,
And Aguilar has sent a kind request,
That we go there awhile to chase the deer.
Now we go not ourself, as urgent things—
And business of the State, make us remain.
Yet it is well we seek the friendship of
Our Spanish friends, because the heathen Moor
Has threatened Portugal with his revenge.
Then 'twill be well to spend a merry hour,
And at the same time, be an embassy.
Thou wilt go, Pedro ; represent ourself,
And say how much we grieve we cannot come.

Be cautious what thou sayst.   Give no pledge,
And yet give courtesy to every one.
My Lord Rudolpho, give your sage advice,
And you my Lord Pechico likewise help.
Pledge not our State to anything, nor give
A guarantee that we shall go to war.

PEDRO.

We go then as ambassadors and friends,
To make fair promises, but give no pledge.
But what if Spain do make a pledge to us;
Shall we accept it, and not give one back ?

ALFONSO.

Give not a pledge, for Portugal seeks not
To mix in wars of Spain, and of the Moor ;
And we shall have full orders writ at once,
What we shall do, and wish our embassy
To do in Spain.

PEDRO.

My gracious sire, your words sound strange to me,
But let it pass.   'Tis better now that we
Get all things ready quickly for the way.

ALFONSO.

Then be your journey happy, light, and gay.
                                        [*Exeunt.*

B

Scene III.—A CHAMBER IN MATTEO'S CASTLE.

Marco, Rodrigo, *and* Alonzo, *sitting at a table.*
MARCO.

Well, good Rodrigo, to-morrow we must hence
to help as best we can our worthy master.   No one
ever heard of the will till the Abbot gave it to Matteo to read.   What did Matteo say ?   Was he not
very wroth ?
RODRIGO.

Yes, verily, he was.   You could not think him
pleased, that, ere he knew thereof, he was a beggar.
I do not understand it, Marco, on my soul I don't,
and 'twixt ourselves, I deem the will has been
forged.
MARCO.

To-morrow is the last day of the trial, and something better may come of it.   But Ludro is astute
and very crafty to guard his speech.   Alas ! I grieve
but for our fair young mistress.   What do you think,
Alonzo, of this matter ?

ALONZO.

The Abbot knows his own affair.   But there is

one about this castle, I mean Sebastian, a fellow who is every where, knows every one, and every thing, and who anon fills your ears with silly talk. Now, he most gravely told me, that he saw the Abbot write this will, and heard him con it over as he wrote it. To-morrow ends the trial, and if justice holds her own, we'll all be merry once again.

Enter SEBASTIAN *as a clown.*

SEBASTIAN.

Good morrow, friends.—I think I heard Alonzo say that master may lose his cause. Well, what an we do! Many a man has lost as good a cause!

MARCO.

But if he lose the suit, he loses all, and we lose home and master. Now, if we lose, Sebastian, whither shall we go?

SEBASTIAN.

Nay, trouble not thy brain, thou hast not much. I straight shall go to heaven.—Wilt thou come with me, Marco?

MARCO.

Yes, an thou leadest the way.

SEBASTIAN.

Then take me by mine hand, and go with me,

and when thou passest heaven's gate, let go mine hand. Then Marco shall see suns, and stars, and angels.—What of mine offer ? Wilt thou go ? Wilt thou go ?

MARCO.

I seek no better company than thyself, Sebastian. But how shall we know heaven, when we get there ?

SEBASTIAN.

I'll teach thy brainless pate. When thou goest with me, thou wilt come to a certain land, where thou wilt see blue heaven above thee, and all around thee, and this earth will be beneath thy feet. Then thy journey will be ended.

MARCO.

An that be so, I am in heaven now.

SEBASTIAN.

As much as thou wilt ever be, so think thyself a saint ; Saint Marco, good Saint Marco !

MARCO.

Now I am a saint, what wilt next make of me ?

SEBASTIAN.

Nothing but what thou art. Here, take my coat

and put it on thy back, and don my cap, and prove
thyself a —— fool ! [*Exit.*

RODRIGO.

Well, an he be a fool, he hath some wit. To-
morrow we shall have more work to do. How I do
fear this trial, yet I shall stay with my master, come
what will of it. Then let us all be with him.

None had ever a better master and mistress, so we
shall stay with him. Let us all remain.

Re-enter SEBASTIAN.

SEBASTIAN.

Aye, let us all remain. But Marco is a saint on
earth, likewise the greatest fool, which is his greatest honour. If master gain, we need not change our
lives. But let us hence.

ALL.

Aye, let us hence, and heaven protect our master.

SEBASTIAN.

And keep Sebastian clear of all disaster.

[*Exeunt.*

Scene IV.—LUDRO'S PRIVATE ROOM IN THE ABBEY.

LUDRO *alone.*

LUDRO.

To-morrow tells the tale.   I must withhold
Myself in every point, and register
Mine actions carefully.
Sancho was witness of this signature ;
But if he dare refuse what I command,
Or doth not swear this will is truly drawn,
Sealed, signed, delivered unto me—and given—
In proper form, and ready for the proof,
I know to do, precisely as I know.—
Matteo !   Simple fool !—his honesty—
His loud-mouthed threat'ning, and his blustering
　　　　mood,
Saying this deed is but a forgery !
I hold it now.   Let him produce his proof !
What shall be done with Inez ?
　　　　　　　　　　A nunnery
Of the most strictest sort, shall hold her from
The world in solitude.   There let her die.——
I'll find a friend to keep Matteo still.——

　　　　　(Draws his dagger and looks at it.)

Aye, thou shalt be my friend !   Thy friendship now
I ask not : but when presently I crave
Thy keen blue point, to rid me of my foe,
And send thee, silent forth to work for me,
Thou shalt not gender wroth, but quickly send
His curdling blood around his quivering heart.——
Then so much for Matteo ! !
Wherefore the use of potions, or the leech
To medicine every silly knave to death—
When surer, and more quiet mode is here.
Go, give a man a potion and he'll roar
And rave, and tell a thousand secret things,
And all around shall know all that he knows.
Nay, if he thinks he's poisoned, he will talk ;
And shivering, tell the gaping crowd around,
Each secret that the world should never know.

    (Holds out the dagger, addressing it.)

But when thou goest to do a deed alone,
Thou carriest not a loud-mouthed prating tongue.
Thou art so still, no mortal knows thy tread,
Nor hears thy breathing, ere he feels thee sting.
Thy foe sees not thy coming nor thy shade,
Nor fears thy tusk, until he feels thee bite !—
My honest, silent friend, go—seek thy rest.

    (Replaces the dagger.)   [*Exit.*

    Enter SEBASTIAN, *stealthily.*

        SEBASTIAN.

He's gone, and thinks his wicked game secure.

Perchance he may be, but I have my doubts ;
Yet, lack-a-day, I have no doubts at all.
Nathless I must be cautious in my acts.
I must secure this will at any price ;
I know the secret passage to this chamber,
And have the honest, secret key for that.

(*Tries to open the desk, but cannot.*)

Not thus, mean I, to end my master's task.
Oh, honest Ludro !   Thou and thy dagger !!!
Hadst no doubts, Ludro, in thy honest breast,
That some vile caitiff might o'erhear thy thoughts—
Yea, verily such a caitiff as myself.
I have grave doubts thou hast been overheard ;
And graver doubts, thou'rt not an honest man.
But therefore I have yet another doubt,
That he will find his bow-string hath a knot,
Who lays such schemes, to serve such villainy.
Oh, honest Ludro, I shall watch thee well.
And I may teach thee such a lesson yet,
That thou shalt learn to doubt, when least in doubt.

(*A noise without.*)

Some one comes hither, and I must away.

(*Holds up the key.*)

My honest silent friend, go seek thy rest.

(*Pockets it securely.*)   [*Exit.*

SCENE V.—A COURT ROOM.

JUDGE, MATTEO, LUDRO, SANCHO, *and* ATTENDANTS.

JUDGE.

My Lord, I must give this cause against thee.
The will is most carefully done, and witnessed in
court. I must give this cause against thee. Thou
hast no witness as the Abbot hath, to prove his claim.

MATTEO.

Witness, most worthy judge !—Witness of what ?
The devil can find witness as he lists,
And then may claim our worthy friend the monk.
As I have said, none reckoned on a will.
None ever heard about such document,
Until my uncle died. Witness, good sooth !
I here declare that all their oaths are false.
But if I am to lose mine heritage,
By baseness, and this Abbot's forgery,
It can't be helped my lord, most certainly.

LUDRO.

I must deny myself, but, had I been
Not thus in harness, as thou see'st me here,

Bound to refrain myself in everything,
Not tamely had I borne my lord's affront.

MATTEO.

Thy garb I do respect, but hate the knave—
That shelter seeks, beneath that decent garb.
Little care I, an it had been myself.
Mine only sister, what can she endure,—
What would my father, or mine uncle say,
Or our loved mother, rising from their tombs!
Methinks they'd point their bony hands at thee,
And from the eyeless sockets of their skulls,
A cold unearthly glare would pierce thee through,
And chill the marrow in thy perjured bones.

JUDGE.

Take heed unto the bridle of thy tongue,
Most noble sir, nor thus revile i' the court.
He holds the will, which gives him this estate;
And I adjudge him, as the writing saith.

LUDRO.

Didst thou not see this will signed, Sancho?

SANCHO.

I saw it signed with mine own eyes.

LUDRO.

Didst thou see it delivered unto me?

SANCHO.

Most surely sir, I did.

LUDRO.

Dost hear what Sancho says on oath, my lord ?

MATTEO.

Dost thou suppose I have not got mine ears ?

LUDRO.

Nay but I do ! so let me counsel thee,
To serve the king, and fight against the Moors.
Go, send fair Inez to a nunnery,
And that will ease this burthen on thy mind.

MATTEO.

Yea truly, that would be a glorious deed !
Now listen what I say !   When I require
Sage counsel from thee, 'twill be time to ask
Thy lying tongue to speak.   How I do loathe thee.
Go, get thee to thy beads, and bless thyself.
Sooner than Inez should become a nun,
I'd rather see her cold, and stiff in death.
A nun, forsooth !—My lord, I leave your court ;
And if this villain Ludro cross my path,
Let him look well, to see himself prepared.

[Exit.

LUDRO.

Oh, let him have full measure with his tongue,
And froth upon the bit.   I hold the reins.

JUDGE.

Now my lord Abbot since thou'st gained thy suit,
Could'st thou not something do, as if by grace,
To let the Lady Inez have a part.
'Tis very hard for her to lose her home.
'Twould be an act most generous, lord Abbot.

LUDRO.

Most noble sir, hearing what thou hast said,
And judging by the Count de Castro's mien,
His passionate address, and foul-mouthed words,
How could I, in regard to mine own self,
Be humbled so as give this woman grace.
For doing grace to her, is grace to him.
This property belongeth not to me ;
But an it did, I'd sooner have it burnt,
Yea rather see it sunken in the sea
Than give one tittle to De Castro's house.
Because I bear this garb upon my back,
Am I to bear reproach unmerited.
Nay, sooner let each quivering limb be torn,
And life's last drop crimson my mangled flesh,
Than I return these Castros e'en one re.
He says I forged this will ! Am perjured too !

Calls me a villain monk, and blackens me,
As if I were a devil, fresh from hell.
Although I am a monk, am I to bear
Each insult that he heaps upon my head !
No my lord judge,—no—never !

(Curtain falls.) [Exit.

SCENE VI.—HALL IN MATTEO'S CASTLE.

MATTEO, ALONZO, RODRIGO, *and* MARCO.

MATTEO.

Now, my good friends, come round me for the
last time. To-morrow I shall leave this castle, and
take me to the mountains. Ye know the dell
where the hermit lived, long years ago. I will go
there to live, and take my sister with me. If fortune favor me I may return again. Now fare ye
well.

RODRIGO.

My worthy master, be not so cast down. We
will not leave thee in adversity.

MARCO.

Good master, we will all remain. Thou canst not
be a servant for thyself. 'Twere folly so to act.

ALONZO.

Does my lord know this cave ?

MATTEO.

I have been to it, but 'tis not enough of size for such a company.

ALONZO.

I know it most truly, master.   There are many caves in it, and some of size enough to hold a thousand men.   So I will guide thee there, and show thee the secret chambers, and the secret well, and the good old hermit's tomb.

Enter INEZ *and* XARA.

INEZ.

Well, my good brother, we have lost our all
But this much we can never lose, Matteo,
Two honest hearts, ever to live and love.
We must endure the lot that falls to us ;
Repining is a craven's act, and vile.
I'll go with thee, wherever thou shalt go.
So let us face the world like honest folks.

XARA.

Dear mistress, wilt thou not let Xara go ?

I am thy Moor, thy honest, faithful Moor ;
And all my life is only bound in thine.

INEZ.

When children, Xara, we together played.
We waded in the brook in summer days,
Or chased the butterfly, or plucked the flower ;
Or wandered, hand in hand along the path,
And joined in merry games, as children do.
My good dear Xara we shall never part.

Enter SEBASTIAN, *out of breath.*

SEBASTIAN.

Oh Lord ! Oh Lord ! what news I have to tell.
Most excellent news—most excellent news.

INEZ.

What is thy news, Sebastian ?

SEBASTIAN.

Well, as I was sitting by the way, I met a company, and being full of wit, I asked who they were and whither they went. And I spoke to a certain nobleman, Lady Inez, and he enquired much for thee, and his name was Pechico, on an embassy to Spain with Prince Pedro. And I told him of thy suit, and he was much grieved, and he told the Prince.

And he promised to look to it. And then he gave
me a piece of gold. Oh Lord! Master Matteo, Oh
Lord! Oh Lord!

MATTEO. ·

What then, Sebastian. Hast found thy breath?

SEBASTIAN.

Then my lord Pechico bid me take Lady Inez this
letter; and he struck me over the back, and gave
me a crown, and he called foul names at me, and
bid me go for a fool. And Lord Rudolpho bid me
run, and he struck me, and gave me nothing'! My
back is all colors. Oh Lord! Oh Lord! And he
said he would see thee anon, Lady Inez. Here, take
thy letter. (*Hands it.*)

INEZ.

Thanks, good Sebastian.

MATTEO.

Thy news is good yet strange, Sebastian.
But we will hence, my friends, and meet
To-morrow at the hermit's cave. [*Exeunt.*

SCENE VII.—THE FOREST NEAR THE CAVE.

MARCO, *seated on a log.*

MARCO.

This is a merry life, I like it every way. We have no horses here to pother with, and a fellow may sit in the sun as he lists. I do nothing since Master Matteo came, but stretch me in the sun. I am too lazy, or I would sing.

Enter SEBASTIAN *behind, with a staff.*

SEBASTIAN (*aside*).

Yonder is lazy Marco. He was always a great one to prate. He is going to sing, so I will get me behind these trees. Sing on Marco. Ho, ho, ho!

(MARCO *rises and sings.*)

MARCO.

1.

When the lark's in the air, and the sun on the lea,
There is nothing I love like mine own companie.
Then I talk to myself of the days that don't last,
And carelessly nod, as I see them run past.

C

Chorus :

Then talk to thyself, boy, and sing whilst thou may,
When thy heart is all merry, it's good companie.

2.

When I'm weary of labor I sit myself down,
And I sing with contentment, when I'm all alone.
And often I think, as I stretch me to rest,
That fellow is wisest who loves himself best.

        Chorus :—Then talk to thyself, boy, &c.

3.

Oh, what need I care for the world as it goes,
As I loll on the grass, or I sing at mine ease.
I have a good master, and that is myself,
And little heed I for the world or its pelf.

        Chorus :—Then talk to thyself, boy, &c.

4.

The courtier may smile and the miser may fret,
But he's happiest far, who his griefs can forget.
So be jolly and gay, as this life you pass through,
And the longer you laugh, you've the less time to
    rue.

        Chorus :—Then talk to thyself, boy, &c.

(SEBASTIAN *strikes him with his staff.*)

Oh ! Lord ! Sebastian, can'st thou not let me be ?

SEBASTIAN.

O Lord ! Marco.   What an excellent voice thou
hast.   But let me tune thee up behind.

(*Beats him off the stage.*) [*Exeunt.*

(*A horn outside.*)   *Enter* MATTEO *and* RODRIGO.

MATTEO.

Did'st hear that horn, Rodrigo ?

RODRIGO.

I did my lord.   But no one comes to chase the
wolf in these wild sierras, that we do know.

MATTEO.

'Tis very strange, and may have import.

(*Horn in the distance.*)

'Tis doubtless some merry huntsman, who retires
with venison enough for a week.   But let us to the
cave.   I promised Inez I would soon return.

[*Exeunt.*

Enter PEDRO, *dressed as a huntsman.*

PEDRO.

Now, this forbodes no good, and yet perchance

It may forbode the very best of luck.
I know I've lost myself among these glens.
But what of that. 'Tis merry to be lost
After the bounding stag. To-morrow comes,
And then the merry gibe, or laughing jest
From comrades round, makes one forget his toils.
But some one hither comes.

Re-enter MATTEO.

(*Both clap their hands on their swords.*)

Dost thou approach me as a friend or foe?

MATTEO.

A question bravely put, and as a man.
A huntsman, an thy garb belie thee not?
We have no quarrel. Wilt thou give thine hand,
And tell me who thou art?

PEDRO.

Most freely, sir, most freely.

(*They shake hands.*)

Prince Pedro, who has come from Portugal,
Upon an embassy to the King of Spain,
Has come to sport awhile with Aguilar.
I'm of his suite, and we set out this morn,
To chase what we could find upon these hills.

In following my hounds in hot pursuit,
I've lost my company, and lost myself.
So, pray, good sir, show me the nearest route,
To lead me home again.

MATTEO.

The day is nearly spent, and many a league
Is now between thee and thy present home.
Come, take such cheer as I can offer thee,
Deer from the hills, and wild-fowl from the lake;
And in the morning I will send thee hence,
With a trusty guide.

PEDRO.

I do accept thy offer.   Courteous sir,
Pray tell me who thou art?

MATTEO.

My name's De Castro, and a noble, too.
Now I'm but an outcast.   Let us hence,
And I will freely speak upon the way;
Telling thee all.
                          [*Exeunt, conversing.*

Scene VIII.—A CHAMBER IN THE CAVE.

Inez *seated on a couch,* Xara *standing beside her.*

Inez.

You know not this stranger, Xara ?

Xara.

I know him not, my lady, yet he seems a very gallant gentleman.

Inez.

And hast thou learnt his name ?

Xara.

Not yet, but I heard Sebastian say he serves in the Prince's company.

Inez.

Who can he be ? His bearing is most noble and courteous. Matteo likes him wondrous well, and every thing he does, is with a grace. He must hence in the morn, to join the prince. Now Xara, when thou art about, learn what thou canst from Sebastian, and keep thine ears and eyes open.

XARA.

He hath brave carriage. What an he were a prince !

INEZ.

Nay ! prate not so, yet presently no doubt he'll tell me all. See, here they come from their repast.

Enter PEDRO and MATTEO.

PEDRO.

I thank thee, lady, for this excellent repast. Hunger makes all men equal. Yet when my ill fortune lost me in the forest, my better fortune found me again, and left me with thee.

INEZ.

Is it the manner of Prince Pedro's company, to flatter every damsel that they meet ?

PEDRO.

I call this day the brightest in my life, and I speak not in parables.

INEZ.

Thou art my guest.—Prithee what is thy name ?

PEDRO.

A name is nothing—I serve the prince, and am called Pedro.

MATTEO.

I must hence to see to mine affairs. Prithee Inez show this gentleman all courtesy till I return, and pardon me for a little space, good sir.

[Exit.

PEDRO.

We are alone, so I will sit by thee, and speak in honesty.

XARA.

Shall I retire, my mistress ?

INEZ.

Yes, good Xara ; and be near if I call thee.

[Exit XARA.

I have two friends that serve your prince, Pechico and Rudolpho. Rudolpho is near of kin. Pechico, though a friend, has not our blood. Dost know them ?

PEDRO.

Two very honest gentlemen, I know them well. Rudolpho, I do truly call my friend. Pechico is more silent in his mood, and keeps his tongue in check; but Rudolpho, like a man, tells thee in honesty, just as he thinks.

INEZ.

Pechico is a friend, and yet I never liked him.

My lord, we are but outcasts for the time ; we have
no home except these dismal rocks; yet we have
human hearts within our breasts, if nothing more
remains.

PEDRO.

Lady, our hearts must ever be our own.   No thief
can steal an honest heart from thee.   Your brother
told me all, and also of the Abbot.

INEZ.

'Twas hard to lose our all ; but happier times will
come.

PEDRO.

I know the prince, and will make mention of it ;
and he loves justice.

INEZ.

Perchance he may but laugh thereat.   A prince at
best is but a gentleman.

PEDRO.

Thou art far fairer to me than proud dames
That I have seen at King Alfonso's court.
Lady, might I present my suit to thee.

INEZ.

Beware to whom you speak ! not likely, sir,

We ever meet again.   I must not pledge
Myself too lightly.

PEDRO.

I ask not lightly, madam, nor a pledge.
But do not spurn a stranger and a guest;
And when again we meet, which soon shall be,
Be not indifferent, I do beseech.

INEZ.

Ere that we meet, perchance some other maid
May take the fancy of my wandering knight.
And yet you seem sincere.

PEDRO.

I am sincere
To thee and every one, and thus I ask,
Thou wilt permit me to return to thee.

INEZ.

I know not what to say, nor dare confess
What seems unmaidenly.   Thou wilt not ask it.
But yet return.   I shall respect at least.

PEDRO.

Thanks, gentle lady, for thy gentleness;
And think there was a stranger once,

Who by those modest cords, unseen, but felt,
Was thus, for ever bound to thee in truth.

INEZ.

Come, if thou wilt. I oft have heard, the Prince
Gives not his countenance to unruly acts.

PEDRO.

Most certainly, and I can swear to that,
For I have known him since he was a child.

(Enter MATTEO.*)*

MATTEO.

I have prepared all things for thee for the morrow,
good sir, and have told that rascal, Sebastian, to
don more decent livery, and be thy guide. But
thou art weary, so let me lead thee to thy couch.

PEDRO.

I would retire my lord, and follow thee. Lady,
good night, and recollect that we shall meet again.

INEZ.

As it may pleasure thee. Good night. Good night.

[*Exeunt,* INEZ *to one side,*

PEDRO *and* MATTEO, *to the other.*

ACT II.

Scene I.— A FOREST.

Sebastian, *in livery of fifteenth century.*

Sebastian.

And I can now return at my will to my master.
This Pedro is a noble gentleman. He gave me three
pieces of gold ; he must have been a gentleman to
do that. A good day's pay ! I shall visit Ludro to-
night, I have the key ; and on the morrow I promised to lead Pechico to the hills. If fortune speed, I
may secure this will; I have promised mine own heart
that I secure it, and verily I keep my promise.—
What an Pechico give me three pieces of gold. Oh,
lucky Sebastian, thou wilt be rich with six pieces of
gold. Good luck, Sebastian ; Good luck to hope for it.

[*Exit.*

Scene II.—LUDRO'S ROOM. *Night.*

Ludro *sitting at his table, the will open, a dagger and bag of gold beside it, lights on the table.*

·˙ LUDRO.

I have the will before me, yet I feel
Not all secure, although I've gained the suit.

(Comes forward.)

If a man venture, he doth something gain ;
And if he venture more, more doth he gain ;
But if he venture over reason's bounds,
Reason forsakes him, and he loses all.
I've ventured, and I've won a broad estate !
This haughty lord De Castro, let him fret,
And grind his soul upon his own regrets.
I am not yet secure, nor can I be,
While he and Inez walk beneath the sun.
'Tis said he's now in some wild mountain cave,
And hath the lady hid ; I'll search him out.
I'll have their bodies soon within my grip,
And with their bodies, I must still their breath.
And when I know they rest beneath the earth,
I'll be in each particular secure.
I now must go to Sancho for a time,
And we shall hatch a modest little scheme
To seize Matteo, and the pretty Inez,
But ere I go, I'll double lock this door.

(Locks the door carefully and Exit.)

Enter SEBASTIAN *stealthily. (He seizes the will and the dagger.*

SEBASTIAN.

I have it, and I'll keep it safely here !

(Hides it in his breast.)

Nay then, worthy Abbot, look to thyself,
Permit no tattling fool like me to hear
The dark communings of thy villain tongue.

(Lifts the bag of gold.)

Oh gold, what art thou ?   Men do sin for thee—
And Solomon says, that thou art still the root
Of every evil wandering 'neath the sun ;
But e'en for that, I wish I had some more ! ! !
A little more could surely do no harm !
This dagger, too, is choicest piece of steel—
Better than mine.   Then, Ludro, I exchange,

(Exchanges daggers.)

Ludro, I'll make thee doubt, my honest monk,
Thou hast those lands—this will secured to thee.
Wilt thou not doubt, when thou returnest here,
That some foul fiend has robbed thy privy cell,
Of will, of dagger, gold and everything ;
Then cram thy stomach till it burst with doubts !
Oh, here they come !—I must retire a while.

[*Retires with the gold, &c.*

Enter LUDRO *and* SANCHO.

LUDRO.

And so thou understandest all I mean.
We travel to the mountains dressed as monks,
To the holy hermit's cell ; but when we come,
Will cast our garments suddenly away,
And slay the two De Castros on the spot.
See that thou hast good weapons belted tight;
Bright blades, and daggers keen, and 'neath thy
    robes
Good armour, to secure each life and limb.

SANCHO.

I'll do thy bidding, sir, in every thing.
I shall prepare a dozen of our herdsmen.
When shall we seek the hills ?

LUDRO.

To-morrow, an thou wilt.

SANCHO.

Nay, 'tis impossible before a week.
We must provide for each contingency ;
But wherefore slay this Inez ?

LUDRO.

Not one De Castro shall impede my way
To heir these broad estates which now we own—
Their ghosts can ne'er return to claim these lands.

SANCHO.

Yet, thou hast heard of most unholy sights ;
Of spirits rising from their loathsome graves,
And seeking vengeance on their murderers ;
Of ghosts that glide around the ruined keep,
And nightly wail, with hollow, dismal moan,
Repenting them of former bloody crimes.
Hast thou not heard, Lord Abbot, of such things ?

LUDRO.

I've heard of many things—of many sights,
And ghostly tales to raise old women's hair,
Or frighten schoolboys.   Hast thou ever heard
Of any gibbering ghost appear in court,
To be a witness in a suit of law ?
I take my chance of ghosts to bother me.

(Turns to the table.)

But where's the will ?   Villain, hast thou that will ?
I left it here just now.   Where is my gold ?
This dagger, too !   Hast thou been playing fool ?

(Holds up the dagger threateningly.)

Now hand them forth, or else this gleaming blade
Shall send thy spirit to the land of ghosts.
Give them me., villain !—Villain, give them up!

SANCHO.

My lord !—my lord !—I nothing know of this !

Have thy fears overcome thy better mind ?—
Perchance thou hast mislaid them for a time
See there—thy desk stands open.

LUDRO.

(*Rushes to the desk.*)

Curse on the gold—that nothing is to me.
But then the deed, the will !———
It is not here, Sancho, it is not here.
Fool that I was to leave it thus alone,
For some foul fiend to spirit it away.
Go, Sancho, haste thee and raise up the house !
Awake each lazy monk, and send him forth
To search the monastery in and out.

SANCHO.

I go with urgent speed.   [*Exeunt hastily.*

(SEBASTIAN *comes forward, nodding his head.*)

SEBASTIAN.

I am the fiend that spirits hence thy will,
And know thy plot against my master's life ;
And I am likewise robber of thy gold !
A very fiendish gentleman am I ;
I'll be so nimble, Ludro, when we meet,
That all thy schemes shall be a gibe on thee.

         [*Exit, holding up the bag of gold.*

D

Scene III.—IN THE FOREST.

Enter Inez *and* Pechico.

Inez.

It cannot be, my lord ! It cannot be.
If I have got a heart, it is mine own,
And at mine own disposal.

Pechico.

Fair Inez, well thou knowest I've loved thee long !
Thy blood is pure, but thou hast no estate.
If thou wilt be my bride, we will away
And seek the castle where my fathers dwelt.

Inez.

Thou offerest, now, thy hand in strangest mood,
Half slightingly, and half with an affront.
But let me tell thee, my Castilian blood
Brooks not affront from haughty Portuguese.

Pechico.

What ! I affront thee ! I throw slight on thee !
Nay, nay, good lady, thou dost much mistake.

Inez.

I know not how. I ne'er returned thy love.

Are there not other ladies in the land
To whom thy vows might sound more pleasantly ?
Then sue no more, and learn to cease to love.
I love another better than thyself.

PECHICO.

And is it thus thou answerest my prayer ?
Then learn, the Portuguese as haughty are
As are Castilians of the best degree,
And tempt me not to seek another mode
Of action towards thyself, and all thy house.

INEZ.

Thou art a curious lover, Lord Pechico,
And be not jealous if I love another.
I like thee as a friend, sincerely so.

PECHICO.

How would'st thou feel, if one you truly loved
Would tell thee that he loved another more ?
I sue for thee, seeking nor land nor gold.

INEZ.

Thou hast my answer, with it be content.

PECHICO.

Then if this be mine answer, let it be !
God wot, 'tis very hard to bear thy words

INEZ.

Adieu, my lord, we must not meet again.

[Exit.

PECHICO.

" Adieu, my lord, we must not meet again."
I cannot say farewell, yet fare thee well.
'Tis better thus to part, as if in hate,
Than filled with sighs and sweet remembrances.
But now a change steals o'er my inmost mind,
Knowing she loves me not ; and such a change !
She loves some other, and my hope is lost.
By heaven, I will not brook her perfidy,
And shall yet have a something like revenge.
But wherefore do I feel myself alone,
And fret, because this woman saith me nay.
I'll love no more.—Revenge ! be thou my friend,
And fill the hollow where my love had dwelt !

[Exit.

Enter XARA.

XARA.

And so my Lord Pechico leaves these hills.
He passed me with a frown upon his brow,
And when he frowns it bodeth something ill.

Enter INEZ (*weeping*).

What aileth thee, my lady ; may I hear ?

INEZ.

It is a grief that wanders with the wind.
Anon 'tis here a moment, and 'tis past.
Pechico pressed his suit most fervently;
But I love Pedro, as I never loved!
Dear Xara, hold thy peace, and let us hence.

[Exeunt, conversing.

SCENE IV.—IN THE FOREST.

MATTEO.

Now tell me truly how thou'st learnt this matter,
art sure that Ludro will be here to kill us?

SEBASTIAN.

My Lord, I was in the Abbot's chamber and heard
him say it. Dost know this? Take it and keep it.
'Tis my proof, and most convincing—(*hands the
parchment to Matteo*)—I give it thee. Then here is
Ludro's dagger made of most excellent steel (*hands
it*); and then to cover my proof, I hand thee Ludro's
purse (*gives it*), and that doth finish it. I likewise
stole his private key one day, and find it an excellent
friend. By our Lady it hath unhinged his villainy

for us. Now my master art thou content with my proofs ?

MATTEO.

Content an hundred fold ! Thanks, good Sebastian for this timely warning; I'll set my men on the watch, and thou shalt be our leader: keep thou Ludro's dagger, 'tis good steel. Prithee didst count his gold.

SEBASTIAN.

I did most certainly. A thousand marks !

MATTEO.

Give me thy hand Sebastian ! The will is here, he cannot forge another ; go then, tell Marco and Rodrigo of it ; keep thy wits about thee, and thine eyes and ears open ; give me thine hand. (*They shake hands.*)

SEBASTIAN.

I will do all thy scheming when we lay our scheme, and that shall be to circumvent this fellow. Yea, I will be merry in the matter, an thou leavest it me ; just leave it to my brain and to my wit, my master. Ha ! Ha !! Ha !!!

MATTEO.

So be it my good friend, Sebastian.

SEBASTIAN.

Had I been a Count I should have run away with
Lady Inez long ago. But I am not a Count, and
therefore did not count thereon.

MATTEO.

Nay, then cease thy silly prate and cease thy
folly ; when these caitiffs do come thou shalt show
thy scheming, and be our leader for the day, and be
my Lord Sebastian and my friend. Verily we will
counterplot them, and thou must plot with me, so let
us hence to tell my followers.   [*Exit.*

SEBASTIAN (*following him*).

Oh, certainly my friend—my worthy and most
honourable friend—my friend, my friend, my most
distinguished friend—whether art thou or I the most
distinguished ! ! ! (*Bows himself off the stage.*)

SCENE V.—THE FOREST

INEZ *and* XARA.

INEZ.

I feel so lonesome. We have nothing here

Except regrets, to feed our weary lives.
How mayest thou feel, Xara ?   Tell me truly.

XARA.

I always feel most happy here, my mistress.
I love to ramble through the mountain dell,
To pluck the wild rose or the eglantine ;
With ne'er a prying eye to watch my steps.

INEZ.

No one can rob us of such simple joys,
For Nature gave them to us at our birth.
Where are those friends whom erst we loved to see ?
And though in solitude, we find delight,
What greater ill than lonely solitude.

XARA.

The time will come that brighter suns may shine,
And then to-day's regrets are but a jest.
But, see, Count Pedro comes, in merry mood.

Enter PEDRO *in hunter's dress.*

PEDRO.

Did I not tell thee we should meet again ?
Dear lady, I have truly kept my word.

(INEZ *advances.   They shake hands.*)

INEZ.

'Tis pleasant, sir, to see a pleasant face.
But one feels lonely in these sombre woods,
With dreamy thoughts within us, that keep pace
With dreary times around, when friends are gone.

PEDRO.

I feel most pleasant when I see thy face.
Nay, lady, 'tis not sweet to see thee sad.

INEZ.

Few friends are with us, save a simple lot
Of old domestics, who have followed us.
But, since this desert is my dwelling-place,
I could be happy if I had one friend
To come at times, and wile away an hour.

XARA (*aside.*)

I'll leave my mistress and this gentleman ;
So let them talk, and weave their cord of love.

[*Exit quietly.*

PEDRO.

In honesty and truth I'll be that friend,
And ne'er repent the evening that we met.
The cave were palace, if but shared by thee.
If thou art sad, oh let me lovingly

Minister comfort, till thy care depart.
Oh, take my heart, my life, all I possess ;
And if the gift be worthy of the name,
Accept it, lady, I can give no more !

INEZ.

I need a friend. I do accept thy gift,
For could I but return thy honest love,
And know that thou sincerely gav'st me thine,
My heart would be content for evermore.

PEDRO.

Then be thy heart content, my own beloved.
For what I give, I give it with my will.
And thus, betrothed, full soon to be my bride,
I'll make thee equal to the proudest dame
That lifts a haughty head in Portugal.
And many a noble yet shall doff his cap,
Standing before thee as his mistress.

INEZ.

My lord, and who art thou?

PEDRO.

Did I not tell thee, Inez, who I was ?
To thee I am but Pedro. To the rest
I am Prince Pedro, and thou art my bride.

(*Clasps her to his breast.*)

INEZ.

Oh, if Matteo's there, to see us bound
As man and wife, I've nothing more to crave.

PEDRO.

Then we will hence, and tell Matteo all.
My lovely bride, God's blessing rest on thee.

[*Exeunt hand-in-hand.*

SCENE VI.—A ROAD IN THE FOREST.

MATTEO, SEBASTIAN, MARCO, RODRIGO, ALONZO, *and
others, armed.*

MATTEO.

How now Sebastian ?   What of thy pilgrims ?

SEBASTIAN.

I saw them coming. They will be here anon.   I
have my pilgrim's staff. (*Holds it up.*)   Wilt thou
sing us a song, Marco ?

MARCO.

My Lord Sebastian, I will sing dumb.   Make
thou these varlets sing.

SEBASTIAN.

Now look ye rascals ; every rascal among you, hold your tongues well in check.   See ye call me my lord, rascals, my Lord Sebastian, and I warrant, we make this Ludro and his crowd, as merry as monks in the vintage.

Enter INEZ *and* XARA.

INEZ.

What meaneth this ado, good Rodrigo ?

RODRIGO.

Sebastian can tell thee, mistress.

SEBASTIAN.

An thou callest me Sebastian, Rodrigo, I will belabor thee soundly.   Call me my lord, fellow,—my Lord ! !   (*Raises his staff.*)

RODRIGO.

My Lord Sebastian !   My lord ! lord ! Oh lord !

INEZ.

Hold Sebastian.—Art thou crazed ?

SEBASTIAN.

Fair lady, I am " my Lord Sebastian " for to-day.

(*Bows very low*).   So call me my "lord."   Down in the vale, seest thou a cavalcade ?   (*Points.*)

INEZ.

I do, (*looks intently*) and it seemeth a company of pilgrims.

SEBASTIAN.

They come to cut thy throat, and Xara's throat, and all our throats.

XARA.

(*Looking*), Thou art crazed, Sebastian.   They are pilgrims, and I see them.

SEBASTIAN.

Now listen, wench.   Call me, " my lord," or I will belabor thy carcass soundly. (*Lifts his staff.*)   To-morrow call me as thou wilt.

MATTEO.

I have news most certain, that yonder company are varlets led by Ludro, who come to seek our lives, and mask themselves as monks.   Sebastian will be leader for the day, and be our master.   My Lord Sebastian !

(SEBASTIAN *bows very low.*)

XARA.

What ! a clown like Sebastian ⸲

SEBASTIAN.

Call me " my lord," or I will shake thy head off of
thy shoulders.   (*Shakes her.*)

XARA.

Oh, my lord ! lord ! lord ! Lo-r-r-r-r-r-r-r-d !   Oh !

(SEBASTIAN *bows to her very low.*)

(*Aside*) Oh, you brute.

SEBASTIAN.

Now my merry men all, hide in the cave, and I
will lead this Ludro in, and then bind ye his hands
behind his back. I next shall lead the others as I list.
See ye all call me "my lord," rascals. (*Exeunt omnes.*)
Come hither, Xara, and help me to don my pilgrim's
coat.

XARA.   (*Assists him*).

Let me bind this cord around thy waist. See they
are coming.   [*Exit.*

SEBASTIAN.

Now I must move myself.   Here comes Ludro.

Enter LUDRO *and company.*

LUDRO.

Thou art a pilgrim, judging by thy garb, who has
been to the hermit's cave.   Dost know the way ?

SEBASTIAN.

I am, and have been to the cave, and now would get me home again.

LUDRO.

Wilt thou lead the way for us ?

SEBASTIAN.

I will lead thyself first, my master, and thou canst lead thy company afterwards.

LUDRO.

Remain my friends ; I will return anon.

Exit following SEBASTIAN.

Re-enter SEBASTIAN.

SEBASTIAN.

Your master told me to lead one Sancho, and four of your company.

SANCHO.

Come with me, four of you.

[*Exeunt, following* SEBASTIAN.

Re-enter SEBASTIAN.

SEBASTIAN.

Now my good friends, follow me, and draw your
beads and pray.

(*He leads them out.*)

Re-enter MATTEO, INEZ, *and* XARA.

MATTEO.

Bravely done, Sebastian !   Bravely done !

Re-enter SEBASTIAN *and servants, guarding* LUDRO,
and his company, who are bound.

SEBASTIAN.

(*Removing his cowl and dress slowly.*)

And so good fellows, your pilgrimage is over.   See
you this company, Lady Inez ?   They come in armour,
to slay thee and all of us.   I'll hang them in an oak,
and they will make fine acorns for the crows.

LUDRO.

We brought our weapons to defend ourselves from
thieves, such as thyself, and De Castro.   But ye shall
pay for this.

SEBASTIAN.

Strip them, and take their armour, and their weapons.   Come hither Xara ; help me to unbuckle this

good Abbot. Dost expect to go to heaven, Ludro, with a dagger by thy side and thy harness on thy back? (*Draws out the dagger.*) Where got'st thou my dagger, rascal? Thou art a mighty warrior, when a woman strips thee.

MATTEO.

Seest thou this parchment, Ludro? (*Shows it.*)

LUDRO.

What! The will! How camest thou by that? 'Twas stolen, none knows how. Thou'lt dearly pay for this.

MATTEO.

Never again shalt thou lay hands on it. 'Tis but thy forgery, and I have proof of it.

SEBASTIAN.

Seest thou this dagger, Ludro? (*Holds it up.*)

LUDRO.

Am I thus bound, to bear each villain's gibe!
Sancho, mark every thing thou seest here,
And bear the impress on thy memory.

SEBASTIAN.

Knowest thou this purse, Ludro? (*Shows it.*)
E

LUDRO.

The will, the dagger, and the gold !   What means
This witchery !   Villains unloose my arms !
Will no one cut these bonds ?   (*Struggles.*)

SEBASTIAN.

Bear thy bonds like a Christian.

LUDRO.

And who art thou ?

SEBASTIAN.

I am a rogue, a jester, and a fool.
Art thou not doubly fooled, and by a fool,
Thou and thy friends ?   I knew of thine intent,
And told my master ; for two friends told it me.

LUDRO.

Thy friends !   'Tis false I say, in everything.
Tell us their names ?   Oh no, thou canst not.

SEBASTIAN.

Mine ears were my two friends.

LUDRO.

Yes, but who told thine ears this prate ?

SEBASTIAN.

A worthy gentleman, whose name is Ludro !
Go, forge another parchment at thine ease ;
Make Sancho swear thy proof, and steal our lands.

LUDRO.

An there be any law in Portugal,
Thou'lt need it all to keep thy neck secured.

SEBASTIAN.

Look to thine own ! Alonzo, tie these rascals in a
string. Put Ludro first; he is the prince of rascals.
See ye belabour them hotly, on their road. Spare
them not on my account.

ALONZO.

My lord Sebastian, give me thy staff.

SEBASTIAN.

Aye, take it (*gives it*) ; now send them on their
way with your merry staves. Spare not this Abbot.
Go at them rascals ! Hie them on their road.

> (MATTEO'S *men beat them off the stage, all
> kicking and shouting.* SEBASTIAN *shouts
> after them.*)

Spare them not for me. Lord, how they run ! I
will follow and see the sport.   [*Exit.*

INEZ.

They came to take our lives, and thou hast sent them back, a laughing-stock for all Castile.

MATTEO.

Now they are gone, we must seek another refuge. But dost remember, Inez, that to-morrow is thy wedding day.   Then thy husband can look better to thee.   We must be secret, till he proclaims thee openly.

INEZ.

Can a maid forget her marriage day, Matteo ?

XARA.

My lord, will they not return to murder us ?

MATTEO.

No fear of that, Xara.   Dost thou too remember to-morrow ?

XARA.

It is my lady's wedding day, to-morrow,
And I shall bid good by to care and sorrow.

(Curtain falls.)

END OF ACT SECOND.

ACT THIRD.

Scene I.—PALACE OF ALFONSO.

An Ante-chamber, Pechico *standing and meditating.*

PECHICO.

I am contemned by this Castilian maid.
She is an outcast !—I,—a nobleman.
She holds no lands, nor anything on earth,
And yet she doth despise me in her soul.——

Enter LUDRO, *unobserved by him.*

Would that I knew her favoured lover's name,
I'd find a mode to make the fellow rue.—
There is the Lady Pauline from Oporto,
I know she will not frown upon my suit.—
Who is this fellow Inez favours thus ?

LUDRO (*advancing*).

Beware, my Lord Pechico.—Have a care
Thy rival doth not overmaster thee.

PECHICO.

What! Ludro here!—I did not see thee enter.

LUDRO.

It matters not. I warn thee to beware!

PECHICO.

Nay, tell his name. I warrant my discretion.

LUDRO.

Beware, my lord! nor let thy choler burn,
Until thou scorch thyself.

PECHICO.

Am I crazed? Tell me this fellow's name.

LUDRO.

The "fellow" is thy Prince—Prince Pedro, sir.—
Did not I warn thee to be circumspect?

PECHICO.

It cannot be! The Prince is, certes, mad!

LUDRO.

Nay, not so mad as thou art.——

PECHICO.

If thou dost tell me truth, I am undone.
But if our noble Prince espouse the dame,
'Twill be small loss to me.——
But to be spurned, doth let an adder loose,
That stings the marrow of my inmost mind.

LUDRO.

Now thou dost speak as doth become a man!
For wantonness she doth prefer the Prince;
So take such satisfaction as thou canst.

PECHICO.

I bear a feeling I can ne'er express.
I hate her now, because I loved her once.
I would not injure her for all I own,
Yet, I could torture her till horror starts!
I hate, I love, and I despise her more.

LUDRO.

Pechico, thou art jealous in thine heart.
Is there a demon ever sprung from hell,——
That is more potent than deep jealousy!
Wouldst thou but see that demon of thy mind
Standing before thee, as a spectre grim.
His face is pale, save when a hectic fire
Burns in his eye, or flushes on his cheek;
His lips are thin and parched—his breath is hot—

He moves with slouching pace—his bosom heaves
And toils with agony, with rage, with love—
In fear's black caldron, smoking with despair !
Then, mark ! within, the fiery serpent hisses,
And with the flame that rises from its eyes,
Keeps that black caldron boiling ever more.
Then see, Pechico, how his body shakes !
How the legs tremble ! On his visage hangs
A ghastly grin, as if flung there by chance.
He clutches in his grasp a broken blade,
And, craven in his heart, dares not to strike.——
Pechico, what think'st thou of this foul thing,
Thou dost embrace, as thy dear, bosom friend ?

PECHICO.

Thy words seem strange to me, and meaningless.
Has she not spurned me from her, as beneath
Her dignity ; and she is penniless !

LUDRO (*Aside*).

I have him, and I'll humour his revenge,
And turn his malice to mine own account.

(*Aloud.*)

And now, my lord, wilt thou my counsel
    take ?
Yet, I beseech, think not I would intrude.

PECHICO.

My worthy friend, how wouldst thou act i' the
 matter ?

LUDRO.

Then listen.   Be a man—act as a man,
And cast aside this drivelling nothingness.
Become a man, and vengeance seek with this——

(*Holds out his dagger.*)

PECHICO.

Give me thine hand.   Wilt thou assist me ?

LUDRO.

Freely !   But be not rash !   Content thyself
Till we do form sure plans to act upon.

(*They shake hands.*)

PECHICO.

Thou makest my heart to steel itself once more.
I promise thee, my friend, that we shall act
In the best accord.   I'll meet thee presently.

[*Exit.*

LUDRO.

He gives himself to be mine instrument ;
And I shall use the fool as pleasures me.

One word had filled his heart with tenderest love,
And but a word—'twas filled with keenest hate.
Such is mankind upon the face of earth—
They are the fools, of fools, who deeper think. [*Exit*

Scene II.—A BANQUET SPREAD IN THE FOREST.

INEZ, ISABELLA, PEDRO, *and* RUDOLPHO *seated*, XARA *and attendants in waiting.*

RUDOLPHO.

A week has gone, my Prince, since thou wast wed.
The circumstance of nations and the state,
Demand our presence at thy father's court.

PEDRO.

My lords, I do agree.   What says my Princess ?

INEZ.

Most surely would I press that thou remain'st,
But it were wrong.   So go, my gracious lord.
When next we meet we'll be the happier.

PEDRO.

'Tis well, my Princess, and I am content.
But thou must leave this cave and wilderness,
And have a kindlier home to dwell within.
Matteo, thou dost know my castle, girt
With orange groves, upon the Tagus' banks ;
Conduct her safely to Mohilla's towers,
With her attendants, and I'll give to thee
That castle, with its lands to be thine own.

RUDOLPHO.

My daughter, go with her, she is thy Queen,
And future Queen of sunny Portugal.

ISABELLA.

I'll strive to make her happy, sir, until
More joyous hours shall lead us to the court.

PEDRO.

I love thee, Inez, and have told thee all ;
Be not cast down, although an adverse wind
Blow bitterly upon our present lot.
Remember, when the storm is past away,
The sun will shine more brightly.

RUDOLPHO.

When doth it please the Prince that we depart ?

PEDRO.

When thou art ready, thou canst marshal us.
And I procured a high command for thee,
Brother Matteo, from the King of Spain.

MATTEO.

Thanks, gracious Prince ; and if it be my lot
To fall in battle 'gainst the heathen Moors,
I'll be content that Inez has a home.
To-morrow I shall lead my sister hence.

RUDOLPHO.

Matteo forces me to act at once.
Commend me to such honest, active men !

PEDRO.

When a man acts, his actions prove the man.

Enter SEBASTIAN, *in haste.*

Well, Sebastian, what's thy errand ?

SEBASTIAN.

A horseman on the way, pricks at full speed, and
I have run to tell it.

RUDOLPHO.

I will meet him.   Matteo, keep a guard.   [*Exit.*

INEZ (*aside to Isabella.*)

I see him, and he is mine enemy.
Keep still, and I will tell thee presently.

ISABELLA (*aside.*)

Thine enemy !   And who can be so base ?

Re-enter RUDOLPHO *with a parchment.*

RUDOLPHO.

Pechico comes, good Prince, with thy recall.

PEDRO.

Pechico comes !   He left our embassy,
And now comes pricking back, with my recall.
Matteo, keep a guard, and keep thy word ;
I'll hence and meet Pechico.

[*Exeunt omnes.*

Scene III.—HALL OF STATE IN THE PALACE.

Flourish of trumpets. Enter King *and* Queen, Suarez. *Lords-in-Waiting, guards, &c. They take their places.*

ALFONSO.

Have we no mention from Navarre ?

SUAREZ.

Urgent, your Grace. The Princess will attend
Such time as thou mayest choose, for her espousal.

QUEEN.

My liege, I hear Prince Pedro will not wed.

ALFONSO.

Oh, very likely, madam, boys will talk.
We'll find due means to deal with him.

QUEEN.

If he do lay his mind upon a scheme,
I'd lay my life he will perform it.

ALFONSO.

Oh, very likely, madam ; (*aside*) so wilt thou.

QUEEN.

But if the Prince refuse the Princess's hand,
Are we, my liege, to suffer contumely ?
Are all in Portugal, and in Navarre
To be affronted by his boyish whim ?

ALFONSO.

We're not prepared to argue such a point.
Time will do more than talk !

QUEEN.

Doubtless it may with some.   Were I a king
I'd make my children *do* as I *command*.

ALFONSO.

Oh, very likely, madam.   (*Aside*) I know that.

QUEEN.

I'd act decidedly, nor brook delay.

ALFONSO.

Oh, very likely, madam.   Now, my lord,
What further business ?

SUAREZ.

The Abbot of Cintra hath a cause, your grace.

ALFONSO.

Let him appear.

Enter LUDRO, *saluting.*

Now, my Lord Abbot, let us hear thy suit.

QUEEN.

My liege, force thou Prince Pedro to espouse
This royal Princess, of a noble race.
And put thyself, a young man, in his place,
Would sense not tell thee, to accept her hand.

ALFONSO.

Oh, very likely, madam. Where's thy proof
That the Prince will not wed ?
But in the meantime, let us hear the suit
Of my Lord Abbot. Speak on, my lord.

LUDRO.

My liege, I lay complaint 'gainst Count De Castro.
His uncle died, leaving his whole estate
As an inheritance unto mine abbey.
This Count De Castro said the will was forged,
And tried the matter in a court of law.

Justice was ours—of course we gained the suit.
My Lord De Castro then secured the will,
And with it, stole a thousand marks in gold.
I ask that justice may be done to me!

QUEEN.

Thou speakest of De Castro.   What of his sister?

LUDRO.

She helped i' the theft, and by report 'tis said,
Hath got the Prince securely in her toils,
As his paramour.——

QUEEN.

The Prince!—Prince Pedro—and his paramour!
A robber's sister.—No! it must be false.

ALFONSO.

Thou joinest these two Castros with our Prince.
Be circumspect!   What proof hast thou of this?

LUDRO.

I am particular my liege.   I said
That such report floats on the air.

ALFONSO.

Report! report!   There's nothing in report!——
In every action it requireth proof.

F

QUEEN.

If this monk come to lie, we'll have him hanged.
If proof be shown for everything we do,
'Tis very little kings would ever do.

ALFONSO.

Oh very likely, madam.　Do thy will.
Go, get this Abbot hanged, then look for the proof.

QUEEN.

(*Looking defiantly.*)

I come not here to bandy words my liege.
The Prince is for the moment led astray.

ALFONSO.

Oh very likely, madam.　Where's thy proof?

(*Noise without.*)

Go, see who waits without.

[*Exit attendant.*

QUEEN.

Your Grace doth know he is a wayward boy.
To have a robber's sister for such use,
Doth bring disgrace upon our royal house;
And it will make Navarre, and Spain, and France,

Raise up their fingers, as they point in scorn.
How canst thou bear to hear such vile report ?

ALFONSO.

I've heard much in my time, and hearing, I
Have learnt due caution in these state affairs.
It were unkingly to be much enraged.

[Re-enter ATTENDANT.

ATTENDANT.

My Lord Pechico waits without, my liege.

ALFONSO.

Pechico ! Usher him at once.

Enter PECHICO, *saluting.*

My lord, what of the embassy, and of the Prince ?

PECHICO.

The Prince and embassy are now arrived.
There is a rumor, and it seemeth true,
That the Prince hath espoused a lady, come
Of noble blood, a Countess of Castile.

QUEEN.

Espoused, my lord Pechico !—Tell it not !

Has the Prince sunk himself beneath his house ?
Oh no, it cannot be ! It cannot be !

(*Wrings her hands.*)

LUDRO.

May it please your Grace, the story is not new.
My lord Pechico would have married her,
But he revolted at the very thought.
And now my liege, it is a certain fact,
That all believe the Prince is surely wed.
I do believe, on my honour, madam.

QUEEN.

Is it not something most unnatural,
To see a prince, in such a woman's grasp.
But if 'tis so, and heaven forbid it be,
I'll use all means presented to my hands,
To rid the earth of such a villain stain.
My lord Pechico wilt thou come anon,
And bring this noble Abbot with thee too ?
Your Grace, I leave your presence.

[*Exit* QUEEN *and her attendants.*

SUAREZ

My liege, what more dost thou command ?

ALFONSO.

We hold to-morrow's court, and then shall tell.
Now we will hence.

(*Flourish of trumpets.*)

[*Exeunt omnes.*

Re-enter LUDRO *and* PECHICO.

LUDRO.

We are alone.   Pechico have a care,
Nor mar our vengeance for thy silly love.
Thou shouldst have told the Quéen an hundred lies,
And raised her passion till it boiled again.
Think what thou art, and pledge thee to revenge !
Art thou a noble, who hath honour left ?——
Art thou a lover, who hath feelings dear ?
Art thou a fool, to cringe to contumely ?
Art thou a man ? then bear not such affront.——
I swear to thee, to keep my vengeance hot ;
To spare not from remorse, nor quit my scent,
Till I do follow to the bounds of earth, and slay
    them.

PECHICO.

I swear to be with thee !   Art thou content ?

LUDRO.

I am content ; we both are well agreed.
Courage Pechico, prove thyself a man ! .

[*Exeunt on different sides of the stage.*

SCENE IV.—A ROOM IN THE PALACE.

QUEEN (*alone*).

QUEEN.

And who is he, to whom I dare confide
The sorrow, that now clings around our throne ?
I will not trust Pechico, nor this abbot;
It seems there is a mist before mine eyes,
So that I nothing sée nor understand;
And my poor soul seems hovering o'er the brink
Of some deep precipice, around whose base
A dismal torrent roars in agony.
Oh, Pedro! am I tortured thus for thee ?
Am I, the Queen of haughty Portugal,
To be debased, because thou art debased?
I yet shall see thee with a royal bride,
Rising untrammelled in thy dignity.—
A robber's sister mates not with a Prince!——

[*Enter a lady in waiting.*

LADY.

Your Grace, My Lord Pechico and the Abbot of
Cintra wait without.

QUEEN.

Admit them. [*Exit lady.*

Enter PECHICO *and* LUDRO (*saluting*).

I pray you, gentlemen, how shall we act
In the matter of the Prince?

PECHICO.

My gracious Queen, the Lady Inez comes,
An offset from Braganza's royal house.
Have her secured, and send her to a nunnery;
As to her brother, hang him if thou wilt.

QUEEN.

And wilt thou undertake to kill him?

PECHICO.

Aye, with a will, most certainly, your Grace.

QUEEN.

What doth our friend advise?

LUDRO.

(*Unsheathes his dagger*).

This speaketh not, nor doth it babble aught,
And I advise this silent comforter.

QUEEN.

I do accept thy silent comforter.
Yet, we require an honest trusty hand.

LUDRO.

I will go and take Sancho for mine helper.

PECHICO.

I am with thee, and take Lorenzo to strike.

QUEEN.

Then go, and do the deed, sheathing each dagger
In its bloody sheath !

LUDRO.

Then let us leave the palace ere the dawn,
And blind all eyes as to our venture;
We know well where they are. And now, your
    Grace,
Let us all pledge to privacy.

QUEEN.

'Tis just.—I take it, that we pledge ourselves.
It is enough; depart and spare her not.—
Wipe out this stain—washing it with her blood !
Then shall Prince Pedro know his mother's will
Is to be reckoned on, before he acts.——

(Curtain falls.)

SCENE V.—THE FOREST.

MARCO, RODRIGO, *and* ALONZO.

ALONZO.

Dost know, Rodrigo, when we must follow our master ?

RODRIGO.

He said he would return to-morrow and tell us.

Enter SEBASTIAN *in haste.*

SEBASTIAN.

Yonder comes a cavalcade of four knights. Do ye know them ?   (*They all look.*)

MARCO

I do. I know Pechico and Ludro too. These fellows come for no good. See, they dismount and tie their horses ; and now they come with murder in their shadows, stalking silently. Go thou, Sebastian, and look to them, and mind thyself ; and we will into the forest, and when they see us not, will steal their horses.

SEBASTIAN.

I must disguise myself, and besmear my features,

I will be circumspect, and lie most hugely. I must get old hosen and a ragged coat over my garments, and be an ancient beggarman. [*Exeunt.*

Enter LUDRO, PECHICO, SANCHO, LORENZO.

LUDRO.

Methinks we're nigh the cave. Now for these Castros.

LORENZO.

It seemeth strange, my lord, no one is around.

LUDRO.

Come, let us careful on. [*Exeunt.*

Re-enter SEBASTIAN *with a staff, as a beggar.*

SEBASTIAN.

I see them coming back. Now for my wit in lying hugely. I will be very deaf, very old, and lie like the devil. . (*Sits behind.*)

Enter LORENZO, LUDRO, SANCHO, *and* PECHICO.

LORENZO.

I cannot find this cave. See, yonder is an old beggar. Come hither, fellow ! He's very deaf.

SEBASTIAN (*Limps forward*).

I am a poor old man, an hundred years of age;
very old, very old !

LUDRO.

Here is an alms for thee, good father. (*Gives it.*)
Dost know the hermit's cave ?　Wilt lead us to it ?

SEBASTIAN.

I do assuredly; I was born here, but it is too far
for my old bones.　Seest thou that rock on yonder
hill ?　The cave is there.　Ye can go without a poor
old man an hundred years of age.

LUDRO.

Art sure the cave is there ?

SEBASTIAN.

It is, master ; and thou wilt find a lady in it with
her maid, and they gave me some meat and wine,
and I came away.　A poor old man, an hundred
years of age.—

PECHICO.

Now our sky looks bright, let us improve the time.

LUDRO.

Inez once dead, my game is nearly played,

LORENZO.

Matteo dead I win, and get my gold. My lord, you promised me a thousand marks.

SEBASTIAN (*in terror, shouts*).

Good master, I have no gold, I swear ! A thousand marks from a poor old man, good lord, a hundred years of age ! O lord, a thousand marks !

PECHICO (*shouts in his ear*).

Thou mistakest, friend. Take this alms.

SEBASTIAN.

May all the saints bless thee for a poor old man, an hundred years of age. May you all be hap—

PECHICO.

Cease, babbling fool ! There's not a moment to be lost. Come, follow me. [*Exeunt.*

(SEBASTIAN *looks after them.*)

SEBASTIAN.

A poor old feeble man an hundred years of age ; a very poor old man an hundred years of age !—Aye, these cut-throats are gone, and I must go too, or they will cut mine likewise. Bravo ! (*he dances lively*), Bravo !! Bravo !!! Now the devil take them. I

will leave them my staff (*plants it in the ground*),
and my hosen and my coat (*hangs them on the staff*),
and now my hat to keep thee from the sun (*hangs
it on*). Ye would be cut throats of a noble lady; if
ye find her not ye will kill this my shadow, and cut
its throat. Oh, poor old man, an hundred years of
age ! Adieu, my lords and gentlemen, adieu !

(*Dances off the stage.*)

Scene VI.—HALL OF AUDIENCE IN THE PALACE.

KING *and* QUEEN *sitting in State,* SUAREZ, RUDOL-
PHO, PEDRO, RAYMOND, *Nobles in waiting,
Guards, and Attendants.*

RUDOLPHO.

My liege, the King of Spain returns thy greeting,
And asked some forces and a subsidy ;
He pledged to send ten thousand men-at-arms,
In case the Moor should enter Portugal.
We promised in return a thousand men,
Likewise five thousand marks in gold.

ALFONSO.

It is not much, a thousand men, e'en less ;
Then have this treaty duly drawn, my lord,
And we shall sign it.   What business next ?

QUEEN

An embassy comes hither from Navarre,
Fraught with much import.

SUAREZ.

Your Grace, this embassy concerns the Prince
And his espousal.

QUEEN.

Your Grace, the Prince is here,—we all are here.
Two kingdoms seek the union.   Let him know
That 'tis thy royal will he be betrothed.
Nay, question not ; have this betrothal made
Secure and binding.

ALFONSO.

Thou art in haste, madam.

PEDRO.

May I not speak i' the matter ?   Am I not of age ?
Do I not know mine own affairs ?

RUDOLPHO (*aside to Pedro*).

Bridle thy tongue, say not another word,
And she will overshoot her mark, and break
Her bowstring.

QUEEN.

Thou shouldst have age enough upon thy back,
To choose thy company, not mate a wench,
The sister of a robber and a thief.

PEDRO.

Speak on, sweet mother.   Hast thou more to say ?

QUEEN.

Yea, I have much.   Accept the Princess's hand,
And every sword in Portugal, each lance
In bold Navarre, shall follow at thy back.

PEDRO.

May it please your Grace, doth the Queen rule this
    realm ?
Is she to scoff at me without a cause ?

RUDOLPHO (*aside to Pedro.*)

Bridle thy choler.   Prick not thine own flesh ;
But let her talk, and flounder in the mud
Of her own argument, until she choke !

QUEEN.

I do abhor to hear unseemly news,
Of thy dishonor, and our own disgrace.

PEDRO.

I'm not dishonored, nor art thou disgraced.
What lying knave has told thee such a tale ?

QUEEN.

Two worthy noblemen, of high degree.
Couldst thou acknowledge her to be thy Queen ?
My Lord Rudolpho, what think'st thou of this ?

RUDOLPHO.

I think, your Grace ?   Thinking ne'er bothers me.
But this I know, that when our noble Prince
Asked the King of Spain, to grant the high command
Against the Moors, unto the Count De Castro,
Your royal friend rejoiced to give it him.
One scarce can call a noble Countess, " wench,"
Sprung from Braganza's race, with royal blood.

RAYMOND.

Your Grace, when I received this embassy,
My King gave orders I should not delay,
But get most certain answer to this matter.
Our Princess is of most commanding presence,
Of beauty rare, and queenly dignity.
I fain would take a cordial answer back.

PEDRO.

Your Grace, before this matter doth proceed,

I ask who told thee of my strange disgrace ?
Because 'tis false in all things !

QUEEN.

My Lord Pechico and the Abbot of Cintra,
Did both declare it.　All men know of it.

PEDRO.

These enemies of mine, and of the Count,
Have told the truth, with her visage strangely
　　marked.
But I will even all my wit to theirs.

RAYMOND.

What says the Prince unto mine embassy ?

QUEEN.

It matters not.　It is our sure command.

RAYMOND.

Then it beseemeth, that Prince Pedro sign
The proper instrument on his own behalf,
And I shall sign it for the Princess.
Here are the proper writings duly drawn.

　　　　　　　　　(*Produces them.*)

QUEEN.

Now my son, sign thy name.
　G

PEDRO.

Count Raymond thou hadst better keep thy scroll.
'Tis folly absolute, to ask of me !
I will not sign my name.

QUEEN.

What sayest thou ?   Not sign ! !

PEDRO.

I'll wed no princess, and will sign no bonds.

QUEEN.

(*Starts up*) Thou wilt not sign thy marriage deed,
    nor yet
Wilt thou act as a prince.   Beshrew me, but
'Twere better I should see thee cold and dead,
Rather than see thee now, before mine eyes,
Casting dishonour on our royal name,
And making us the laughing-stock of all.

RAYMOND.

Prince Pedro, 'tis not meet I ask a boon,
Granted unto Navarre.
Think thou of it, before the deed is signed,
And I will wait till it may pleasure thee.

PEDRO.

Yes, I shall wait till it doth pleasure me.

I tell thee plainly I will never wed.—
Will never sign such claim upon myself.—
Will never call the Princess of Navarre,
My Queen.   This is what I declare to thee !
Ye all do hear my answer.   Fare ye well.

[*Exit defiantly.*

ALFONSO.

My Lords Raymond and Rudolpho, follow him,
And bring him back.   The Prince seems mad !

[*Exeunt Raymond and Rodolpho.*

QUEEN.

Now by the honour of my royal name,
I will not brook defiance from my son.
Had ever Queen such galling vile affront
Cast in her face, before a noble court !
Nay, though he die beneath mine enmity,
I'll force him yet, humbly upon his knee,
To ask my pardon, and to wed the Princess.

Re-enter RAYMOND *and* RUDOLPHO.

My Lords, what of the Prince ?

RAYMOND.

He is the wildest youth I ever saw !
As I, and Lord Rudolpho came, your Grace,

He drew his weapon, bidding us to stand,
Because we asked him to forego his rage;
For, 'twas the King's command that he return.

QUEEN.

Rudolpho, didst thou try him ?

RUDOLPHO.

I did your Grace, and did entreat him sore,
But he did gibe at me—called me a fool,
And said thou wert a devil in a way !
And then he swore, and much abused the King;
Called him a dotard, and your Grace's fool;
Said, he was only fit to groom an ass,
Then ride upon his back, to feed the bears,—
And other language horrid to repeat !
He is distraught your Grace, completely so.

ALFONSO.

We will retire to reason with the Prince.

QUEEN.

What ! Reason with a madman and a fool ?
But I will strike a blow when he thinks not,
And rid myself, and all mankind of her.
He doth affront us in the open court,
And all Navarre, and sunny Portugal !
My royal spouse, what shall we do with him ?

ALFONSO.

Nothing to-night, your Grace, nothing to-night.
Leave it until the morrow.   (*Rises.*)

(*Flourish of trumpets—curtain falls.*)

SCENE VII.—A CHAMBER IN MOHILLA.

INEZ, ISABELLA, *and* PEDRO, *seated,* XARA *in attendance.*

ISABELLA.

Hast thou never seen the Queen, Inez ?

INEZ.

Never in my life.

PEDRO.

Hast thou a mirror ?   Look therein and see the
future Queen of Portugal. I have affronted all
Navarre, for thee.   My darling, I do love thee more
and more.   And when thy reason doth so rule thy
mind, it makes thyself my heaven of living love.

(*Kisses her.*)

INEZ.

If thou art happy I am content, my husband, and I can trust thine honour.

RUDOLPHO (*witho::t, shouts*).

The Prince, the Prince ? where are the Lady Inez and the Prince ?

(*Enters in haste.*)

Thank heaven I am in time. Now hasten hence and save your lives. The Queen approaches to kill you all and burn the castle. She hath an hundred cut-throats. On my estate near Coimbra seek a home.

PEDRO.

Come Xara, help the Lady Isabella; we have no time to wonder and to weep, and when a league is 'twixt us and Mohilla, we can stop to think.

XARA.

(*Unsheathes her dagger.*) I have a friend I carry in my belt, hidden away, and see it.

(*Holds it up.*)

RUDOLPHO.

Come Isabella, and bring Xara forth ; I'll take the Princess and the Prince with me.

[*Exit, all following.*

Enter SEBASTIAN (*noise outside*).

SEBASTIAN.

I see Ludro, Pechico, the Queen, and Sancho.
The Queen is one she-cut-throat with a mask.
This grand apartment is too hot for me,—
For fire, and swords, and fiends, are coming in ;
Black human owls, blacker than any devils !
When they come in, the place must smack of hell ¡

[*Exit.*

Enter the QUEEN, LORENZO, SANCHO, LUDRO,
PECHICO, *and soldiers.*

QUEEN.

They have escaped ! How comes it ! Lorenzo,
search the Castle round. Have every corner seen,
and find their hiding place.   ·
I will not brook such mockery for an hour.
She can't escape me, for I'll follow her
Till I behold her corpse, e'en at the mouth of hell.

[*Exeunt all but* LUDRO *and the* QUEEN.

I feel demeaned because I found her not.

LUDRO.

If I be bold, the fault was with your Grace
In coming here in such a violent mood.—
Nothing can come of it, save disappointment.

QUEEN.

Then give thy best advice, my lord.

LUDRO.

Then let not passionate action be thy guide.
Let none into thy secrets save thyself.
Weave gentle threads around them for a time,
But keep thy vengeance hot within thy soul;
And when they deem their secret place unknown,
Steal on them suddenly, with dagger hid,—
And sheathe it in the centre of her heart.
To do this, taketh time, and earnest thought.

(*Noise without.*)

(*A voice.*) Bring him this way, this way.

Enter SEBASTIAN *bound and very lame, between two
soldiers,* PECHICO, LORENZO, SANCHO, &c.

PECHICO.

We searched most faithfully on every hand, your
Grace, and found only this fellow.

QUEEN.

And who art thou?

SEBASTIAN (*Aside.*).

Now I must lie hugely and act the fool or be hanged.

(*Aloud.*) I was following the others, mistress, for they told me the King would cut my throat, because Lady Inez married Prince Pedro.

QUEEN.

Whither are they gone—tell quickly.

SEBASTIAN.

To Granada, to become Moors.

QUEEN.

To Granada ?   What, the Prince ?

SEBASTIAN.

Yea, to Granada, to become Moors.

QUEEN.

When went they ?

SEBASTIAN.

Yesterday at noon.   They told me to keep the castle, but when I saw these men, I hid away.

LUDRO.

To Granada, saidst thou ?

SEBASTIAN.

Aye, to Granada.   Art thou deaf ?   To Granada, to become Moors.   Xara is a Moor,

PECHICO.

Dost speak truth, fellow ? Art not thou one Sebastian, and how comes thy lameness ?

SEBASTIAN.

Dost know Sebastian ? He is gone with Xara to become a Moor. A very merry fellow, full of lies, and gibes. Dost know Sebastian ? He is my brother. I want mine arms unbound. But I like not the Moors, they lie so.

QUEEN (*aside*).

He seems not very wise (*Aloud*). I will let thee go, but when will the Prince return ?

SEBASTIAN.

I will tell thee, good woman. I heard him swear by Saint Marco, and Saint Louis, and Saint Peter, he would return in a year and a day, and slay one Ludro. Belike I will tell Ludro, an I meet him.

LUDRO.

What else ? Here is a mark for thee, good fellow.

QUEEN.

Unbind his arms. Here is another mark. Now tell me thy name. (*They unbind him.*)

SEBASTIAN.

My brother is a fool, but I am not. So Pedro calls
me, Wisdom, Wisdom. I have no other name.

QUEEN.

Poor wretch! My lords let us away to take another time. I yet will find her out.

[*Exeunt leaving* SEBASTIAN.

SEBASTIAN.

I've lied most hugely! I gained two pieces in
gold, fine profit for my lies. I will be far away ere
daylight. Lies pay well, when the devil is pay-
master. They are gone, and I shall go anon. An a
fellow lie to cheat Ludro and the Queen, as I have,
he must have wit enough to cheat the devil, and I
have cheated these devils, who are worse than
devils, who are worse than Beelzebub.—Sebastian, I
am proud of thee, my son. Thou hast lied mon-
strous. [*Exit, shouting bravo! bravo! bravo! and
clinking the gold in his hand.*

ACT IV.

(A period of nine years is supposed to have intervened since last Act.)

SCENE I.—AUDIENCE CHAMBER IN THE PALACE.

The King seated.   RUDOLPHO and attendants standing.

ALFONSO.

Didst hear, my Lord Rudolpho, of the Queen ?

RUDOLPHO.

I did not hear, your Grace.

ALFONSO.

Thou knowest of Prince Pedro's gentle wife ;
He doth not bring her to our presence here,
Yet doth acknowledge her.   The Queen, one day,
Asked me to give an order for her death.

RUDOLPHO,

Her death, my liege !

ALFONSO.

Aye, for her murder, for it was the same.
Poor Inez, doubtless, truly loves the Prince.

RUDOLPHO.

I am amazed, my liege ! How didst thou act ?

ALFONSO.

Oh, we had learnt the art of being deaf,
Which to a king, is matter of great moment.
When her Grace asks unreasonable things,
I will turn deaf, ask what 'tis of the clock,
Or if she breakfasted. She leaves in a rage
Nor bothers for a time, just as we wish.
Then if some courtier fain would tell to me
Tales that would prejudice another man,
I turn exceeding deaf, and ask the news
Last come from Tripoli, or from the Moon.
He soon departs, and scratches at his ear.
Perchance some other, with much import, may
Declare he hath his duty to perform,
And straightway lays complaint, how such an one
Did say vile things of me, behind my back ;
And maketh such ado thereat. Then I
Do straightway tell him it is time to dine ;
And turning deaf, smile at his strange confusion.
And he doth blush, to know I listen not.
Then if another would inflame my wit,

And set me in a rage, and blazing passion,
I ask, what good doth come of it, to burn
My reason out ! So I turn deaf and laugh.
Then, when my fiery friend doth see me laugh,
He turneth cool, and nothing further prates.
Nay, I turn deaf an hundred times a day !——
Some men have got a wicked craving, sir,
To hear all tales, that do annoy and vex ;
And being vexed, bother their friends around.
Now, an they had been deaf, they had been happy.
Would'st thou be happy, list not bad men's tongues,
But turning deaf, thou hast the greater wisdom.
So then, my lord, from the King to the beggar,
That one is happiest who shuts his ears,
And turneth deaf to all things that do vex.
There is a royal art in being deaf,—
To know the proper moment, properly,
When deafness stoppeth every wicked sound.
Keep thine eyes open. Shut thine ears to tales
That fools do bring, to harrow up thy mind.

RUDOLPHO.

My liege, thou truly speakest reason now ;
Yet one must ponder well, before his ears
Are stopped to every tale that floats around.

(*Flourish of trumpets. Enter the* QUEEN, PRINCE
PEDRO, *and attendants. She takes her seat.*)

ALFONSO.

Your Grace doth honour us by coming here.

QUEEN.

My liege, I fain would honour thee, but now
A great dishonour stains our dignity.

ALFONSO.

I know what thou would'st say.   'Tis of the Prince.
I give no sanction that his wife be slain ;
Her murder would disgrace our name for ever.
What thinks my Lord Rudolpho ?

RUDOLPHO.

My liege, if thou would'st kill each lying knave,
And every woman with a vengeful will,
I doubt some thrones might soon be tenantless.
Husbands would lose their wives, .children be or-
        phans ;
And a general noise be raised in Portugal,
Enough to scare most devils back to hell.

QUEEN.

My lord, I say I understand thee not.
Hast thou the daring thus to beard thy Queen,
And in his Grace's presence ? Have a care,
Or thou mightst see a dungeon, ere thou would'st.

RUDOLPHO.

May it please your Grace, I did not mean affront.

QUEEN.

Affront ! What thrones would then be tenantless?
'Tis us, thou meanest, my lord !
How can we be content to see the heir
Of Portugal demean our royal house
By base associates, and this robber brood.

PEDRO.

How wisely doth my tender mother talk.
What a vile wretch is this unlucky Prince ;
At least he would be, an thy tale were honest.

QUEEN.

Thy tongue doth wag most wantonly, Prince Pedro.
Thou dost insult us, as thou hast Navarre ;
Did not thy minion's brother rob the Abbot ?
Did not this Inez look thereon and laugh ?
Thou hast disgraced thyself, and married her.—
A common harlot is no prince's mate.

PEDRO.

If she were as thou sayest, I'd basely act !
But such mad speech requireth not an answer.
My Lord Rudolpho, wilt thou speak for me ?

RUDOLPHO.

May it please your Grace, the Prince doth no such
    thing.
I know this lady that he fondly loves.—
She carries in her veins, Braganza's blood.
Her father was a noble of renown,
Who lost his life defending Portugal ;
And our good King, did grieve with manly grief,
When told that Count De Castro had been slain.
Perchance your Grace may deign to mind thereof !
Nay, I declare it, that this lady hath
A royal carriage, and a noble grace,
And is more womanly in thought and acts,
Than many a devil in a queenly garb.
And my mind makes me say, to murder her,
Were foulest blot, disgracing Portugal.
And humbly I do say, as doth my King.

QUEEN.

My lord, thy speech is filled with insolence.
We brook not such affront.   Then know, my lord,
Thy presence in this court is asked not.
Go, get thee hence, and come not back again !

ALFONSO.

Your Grace, I'm here.   My lord, thou peakest well
And, as a nobleman, declarest thy mind,
And it agrees with ours.   What says the Prince ?
   H

PEDRO.

My gentle mother genders wicked thoughts.
She hath strange whims and notions of revenge
Upon a lady she has never seen ;—
A lady who has every queenly grace,
Of royal ancestry, and noble birth ;
And who, I here declare, if we do live,
Shall sit upon that throne beside myself.
So now my gentle mother, have a care !
For, had it not been for thine enmity,
Which hath no smell of reason nor of sense,
I should have proudly brought her to this court,
And bid defiance to thy royal rage.
But then, the Princess ne'er would give consent ;
And said, that time would surely bring a balm
To change thine anger into lovingness.—
Yet thou hast sworn to take my lady's life.
But I do plainly warn thee, gentle mother,
See that thou harm'st her not.   For I do swear,—
And in the hearing of my royal sire,—
To follow to the death, woman or man,
Who slays the gentle Inez of my heart.
See that thou hast a care, for I do mean it.
Aye, every word of it, good mother.

QUEEN.

My liege, and dost thou hear such violent words,
E'en in thy presence,—and must I submit

To hear the Prince use threatenings to my teeth,
And be dishonoured, sitting on my throne.
Hast thou not royal dignity enough
To banish from thy court, my Lord Rudolpho ?
I will not brook such ruthless insult.

ALFONSO.

My Lord Rudolpho spake as on his honour.
If your Grace be affronted by his speech,
We think there is no need.   As to the Prince,
He made no threats against thee, nor thy life.
He only said, if man or woman slew
The lady of his heart, he'd slay in turn.
Now I do say, pledging my royal word,
That if thyself was foully murdered, by
The hand of any one upon the earth,
I'd follow him until that he was dead.
So, let us leave this matter till again.
It makes thee choleric withal, your Grace.

QUEEN.

Since then the master, and the servant too,
Do spit upon the lady of the house,
'Tis time I were away.   I go, my liege,
To my confessor, and to pray for thee,
For better reason, and more kingly grace.

ALFONSO.

Many thanks, madam, see thou prayest too,—

" Forgive our trespasses as we forgive."
But prayer is very useful for the choler,
And people being choleric, should pray.
'Tis also useful for digestion.

QUEEN.

I've brooked enough, and I can brook no more !

      [*Exit majestically, with attendants.*

ALFONSO.

She's gone, Rudolpho ! and I'm grieved at heart,
That she doth follow on, so vengefully,
Prince Pedro's wife.   There is a bitterness
About my queen, that seems unwomanly.
But we must hence !

                  (*Curtain falls.*)

SCENE II.—IN THE FOREST OF COIMBRA.

LORENZO *alone.*

LORENZO.

I have been through this forest many a league ;
Have been through every secret path and turn ;
And seen Prince Pedro wandering at his will.

Yes, I can lead the Queen with safety in,
And I do know my business thoroughly.
Pechico is a craven in his heart ;
Ludro, a villain filled with enmity ;
Sancho, a knave, outwitting his base master;
Too great a coward he, to strike a blow.
The Lady Pauline is a passionate dame,—
Fit mate for her good lord, the Count Pechico.
The Queen !!!—the blackest devil of them all !
As to myself, I seek a sustenance.—
I am a soldier, killing is my trade ;
Led on in war, I learned but to obey.
I've pledged mine honour to my paymasters,
And gold alone can bind mine honour to them.
Yonder comes Ludro, scheming with Pechico.
Ludro would kill these Castros for their lands,
For which he hath not e'en the shadow of right:
And the others, from unreasoning hate alone,
Would take the lives of Inez and her sons.
Pechico brings a dozen of his men,
To make secure he kills the gentle lady,
And the vile queen doth bring an hundred more,
To slay two little boys, scarce ten years old.
I loathe such company, but I am hired ;
So I must hence, to meet them presently.

[*Exit.*

SCENE III.—A CHAMBER IN RUDOLPHO'S CASTLE.

INEZ *and* PEDRO, *with* LADY ISABELLA, *seated.*

INEZ.

The Queen doth still persist in enmity.
Are not nine weary years of sun and showers
Enough to dull the fierceness of her hate ?

PEDRO.

Fear not ! thy loving husband is the Prince.
My father's malady turns daily worse.—
I promised him, I should return ere morn.

INEZ.

We all do trust thee, for we all do love thee ;
Yet a strange voice doth whisper in mine ear,
That you and I shall never meet again.

PEDRO.

Cast hence these shadows of a timorous mind :
Matteo will be with us in a month.

INEZ.

Matteo ! I shall never see Matteo.

Dost thou believe in dreams ? I had a dream,
And it remains fixed firmly in my mind ;
So let me ease my heart, and tell my dream.

PEDRO.

Then tell thy dream, my love, 'twill ease thine heart.

INEZ.

I dreamed that I was sitting by a stream,
And all was happiness, for thou wert there.
I saw the blue waves dancing merrily,
When suddenly the river turned to blood !
Behold ! a human hand of giant size,
Bony and gaunt, as of a skeleton,
Rose from the bloody stream and seized on us,
Dragging my boys and me beneath the waves.
I called aloud for thee, but thou wert gone ;
And then that bony hand rose up on high
And vanished on the air !
This dream hangs on my mind, and chokes my heart.

PEDRO.

Think not of it.   It renders all things dull ;
Cheer up ! What sayest thou, Lady Isabella ?

ISABELLA.

It is but some disturbance of her blood.
Come then, sweet Lady Inez, cheer thee up,

See, here come thy two sons, with rosy cheeks,
And all the joyousness of early years.

(*Enter* CARLOS *and* ALFONSO, *running to the* PRINCE.)

PEDRO.

Well, my sons, what sports have ye been at ?

PRINCE ALFONSO.

We had such rare sport ! Carlos hit the mark,
And then I took my turn, and notched his arrow ;
And then Sebastian told us we would be,
Ere long, the finest archers in the realm !

PEDRO.

Well done ! my sons.   Ye both are famous archers.

INEZ.

Come hither till I kiss you both, my boys !
I should be happy with you and the Prince,
If I am ever to be happy more.   (*Kisses them.*)

ISABELLA.

If thou art ever to be happy more ?
What means my lady ?   Thou art happy now !

INEZ.

I should be, but this weight lies on my breast.

PEDRO.

I never saw thee in so strange a mood.—
Thou knowest I must leave thee ere the dawn,
So let us be merry for a little space.
Come Lady Isabel, we will away !

[*Exeunt omnes.*

SCENE IV.—THE FOREST.

Enter QUEEN, PAULINE, LUDRO, PECHICO, SANCHO,
LORENZO, &c., *all-masked.* (*They unmask.*)

QUEEN.

My Lady Pauline, hast thou nerved thyself ?
·I feel within me, we have her secure.
If thou wilt not, myself will strike the blow.

LUDRO.

Then open not thy mouth, nor speak one word.—
Compress thy lips, biting thy nether one.—
Hold thy breath hard, and send thy dagger home.
Can'st thou do this, your Grace ?

QUEEN.

I can dare anything that man can dare.—
I've come to seek her life at any chance.
Now I am here, nor hell shall drive me back !

PECHICO.

Your Grace, I almost fear to go with thee ;
For if 'tis ever known who did the crime,
Vengeance will overtake them fearfully.

QUEEN.

If thou dost act the craven, at the time
That thou shouldst be man in every joint,
Better thou dost return, with thy wife's cloak,
Covering the gallant carcass of my lord.
Hast thou the spirit of a gentleman,
And fearest to go, where two women go ?

PAULINE.

Lag not, my lord ! The nation seeks her blood.—
The greater honour ours, who do the deed.

PECHICO.

Lead on, lead on, I follow to the death !

LORENZO.

Come, I will guide you to this woman's chamber.

            [*They mask—Exeunt cautiously.*

SCENE V.—A CHAMBER IN THE CASTLE.

INEZ *alone (comes to the front of the stage).*

INEZ.

The Prince is scarcely gone an hour ago,
And I do feel we never meet again.
What is this feeling that creeps over me,
Binding my soul, as with the shades of death ?
What art thou, death, with thy pale, lurid lip,
And sunken orbs, that tracks us day by day ?
Unceasingly thou followest where we move,
Until thine icy fingers touch the heart,
Stilling its action for all good or ill.
But I hold that within, the inner life,
Which death approaches not.　Mortals may kill
This mortal body, in its agony ;
And we may sink, unheeded, to the tomb.
But my soul, rising o'er the wreck of time,
Sees earth beneath, immortal skies above ;
And though death stand beside me, even now,
I feel my soul rising above my body,
Leaving this world, for an immortal one.
Aye, though my body moulder in the grave,
And every atom shall return to dust,
I hold within a tinge of Deity.—
'Tis the immortal soul, that God doth give.

When time shall cease to be, my spirit still shall
live.

Enter the QUEEN, *masked.*

And who art thou ?

(QUEEN *unmasks.*)

QUEEN.

Vile woman, dost thou know me ?

INEZ.

How can I tell, whom I have never seen ?

QUEEN.

Then know, I am the Queen, and I have come
To blot thy name for ever from the earth.

INEZ.

The Queen ! Then I am lost, with none to save me.

QUEEN.

I am the Queen ; and now prepare thyself ;—
A little moment and thou art no more.

INEZ.

What have I done, your Grace, to merit this ?
I never injured thee by word or deed,
But I have loved the Prince and our two boys.

QUEEN.

Thy boys ?   Where are they now ?

INEZ.

Both, yonder, are asleep.   Thou wilt not kill them ?
Oh, mercy, lady !   Do not kill my babes !

QUEEN.

When thou art dead 'twill matter not to thee.
Learn, I have sworn to see thy livid corpse—
To kill thy brats and know ye all are dead.

INEZ (*kneels*).

Oh, mercy, lady !   On my knees I ask
That thou wilt spare my children.   What did they—
Or I, or mine, to harm thee or to injure ?
My father died in battle 'gainst the Moors,
And lost his life for thee and for the King !
Take my life freely, lady, if thou wilt,
But spare my innocent and lovely sons !
Poor harmless little things, their father's pride ;
What will he feel when he beholds them dead ?
Will not the big tear drop in agony ?
Take my life if thou wilt, but spare my sons !
Hast thou a mother's feeling in thy breast ?
Oh, lady, spare them, spare my noble boys !

QUEEN.

Hast thou no more to prate about ?   Ho, there !

Enter LUDRO, LORENZO, PECHICO, PAULINE, SANCHO
and others.

Here is this woman ! her two boys are there ;
Now go ye in and bring their corpses forth.
Lorenzo, hold this woman.   (*Inez rises.   Exeunt
except* LORENZO, PAULINE, *and* QUEEN.   *Shrieks and
sobs within.*)

INEZ.

O God, my children ?   Mercy !   Mercy !   Mercy !
Oh, let me kiss them once before I die ;—
My last embrace.—A mother's last farewell.

(*They re-enter with the dead children, and lay them
down.*)

QUEEN.

Are they both dead ?

LUDRO.

Both of them.

QUEEN.

Then kill her, Ludro, and be quick on't.

(LUDRO *stabs* INEZ, *and she falls without a sob.*)

LUDRO.

One blow, 'tis done.   Let us away, before
The sound disturbs the other vipers near us.

(XARA *rushes in.*)

XARA.

Oh, fiends of hell, what have ye done to her ?
Ye have killed my lady and her sons !

QUEEN.

Silence, woman !

XARA.

Silence, thou devil ? They have killed the Princess !

QUEEN (*points to* INEZ.)

Make sure of her, and for a moment watch
Till we escape, Lorenzo.

(*Raises her dagger.*)

Thank Heaven, this woman's dead,
And I am well revenged !

(*Exeunt all but* XARA *and* LORENZO, *who approaches,
looking at* INEZ, *his dagger in his hand.*)

LORENZO.

I'll strike once more before that I go hence,

XARÁ (*unsheathing her dagger*).

Back on thy life, and touch her not.

LORENZO.

Peace, babbling fool !   (*He stoops over* INEZ.)

XARA (*stabs him and he falls*).

Back with thee !   Back, I say !
Is not one wound enough, that her poor corpse
Be so disfigured by thine enmity ?

LORENZO.

And I am as this corpse beside me here,—
A moment more and I am with the dead !
Thou hast but done as I would do to thee,
Brave woman !   Take my gold, and bury me
In some lone spot, where none may see my grave.
I never knew my mother and my sire.—
I leave the world regretted not, nor known. (*Dies.*)

XARA.

Bury thee !   Others may, to hide thy body.

Enter SANCHO, *masked.*

SANCHO.

What dost thou here, Lorenzo, hasten hence.
What! dead—Lorenzo dead ? (*Stoops over him.*)

XARA.

Die, villain, die !   (*Stabs him, he falls.*)
And know the Moorish blood of Granada
Comes rushing through my heart, and bounds
In every vein.

SANCHO.

A curse on Ludro, and upon the Queen,
Curse on Pechico, Pauline, and them all ;
That this disgrace surrounds me in my death.
Slain by a Moorish woman.   Curse on her !
I feel the last drop trickling from my heart,
Disgraced in death, and by a woman slain.
Curse on them all, or I had not died thus.   (*Dies.*)

XARA.

And curse on thee, thou cruel ruthless hound,
To kill my lady and her noble sons.
What had they done, foul wretch, to injure thee,
Or any of those devils in thy band ?
Curse on, and die, and find thy way to hell !

Enter a soldier masked.

SOLDIER.

What a wild scene is here !   I come for them,
And they are dead.   But who hath slain them ?

I

XARA.

(Springs at and stabs him.　He staggers off the stage.)

'Twas I who slew them, and I have slain thyself.
Go thou and join thy brother murderers,
For even hell will spurn them from its midst !

(PEDRO and RUDOLPHO rush in.)

Back, back, ye demons ; touch her not, nor dare
To harm my lady's corpse.—It is the Prince and
My good Lord Rudolpho.　　*(She staggers
　　into the arms of RUDOLPHO, who lays her aside.)*

PEDRO.

O God ! O God ! and we have come too late.
Inez, my darling, have they murdered thee,
And our sweet boys, and Xara.

(INEZ moves and PEDRO raises her.)

RUDOLPHO.

Give her more air ;　see, her eyes open.

PEDRO.

Would we had come in time ;　this bloody scene
Had not been acted.　Oh, my wife, my sons !
Have ye all gone, and left me desolate !

RUDOLPHO.

Canst thou speak, lady ?

PEDRO.

But one word, Inez, but one little word ?

RUDOLPHO.

Here is some water, place it to her lips.   (*Does so.*)
Methinks she gathers e'en a little strength.
Be very gentle with her,—very gentle.

PEDRO.

It is the last spark of the dying lamp,
That flickers for a moment, and is stilled.
Look in mine eyes, and when thine eye meets mine,
Perchance 'twill help to warm thy mind again.

(INEZ *clasps her arms round his neck.*)

INEZ.

And thou art come to kiss me ere I die :—
To clasp me tenderly ere I depart.
Our children sleep together, side by side ;—
Lay me beside them, and I'll sleep in peace.
Pedro, mine own, wilt thou not sometimes think
How we did love each other tenderly.
Heaven bless thee, Pedro !   Kiss me ere I die.
                              (*They kiss.*)

XARA *comes forward,*

XARA.

She is not dead,   I hear her voice again.
I have avenged thy blood, and bitterly.
My lady, dost thou know me ?

(INEZ *looks at* XARA, *and nods her head.*)

INEZ.

Be kind to my good Xara and Sebastian.
They loved us all, and served us faithfully.

RUDOLPHO.

Thou mayest recover yet, so cheer thee up.

PEDRO.

Xara shall never leave me, nor Sebastian.

(*Kissing her.*)

Then, Inez, cheer thee up, thou wilt not die.
This bitter cup of death will pass away,
And thou shalt live to be my loving queen.

INEZ.

(*She points her finger to the air.*)

Our children beckon that I come away.
Dost thou not see them, Pedro, with a light,

Brighter than is the sun, around their brows ?
They call on me.   Dost thou not hear them speak ?
Kiss me once more (*does so*), but thou art turning
    dim,
And passing from me, as they brighter grow.
But I will yet return, to be with thee,
To bring thee peace, and be thy comforter,
And we shall live forever with our God.——
Mine eyes are dull.   I go to them.   Farewell !

                              (*Dies.*)

          RUDOLPHO.

O, Lady Inez, thou art gone forever !
And thus the hellish spite and foul revenge
They dare not cast on him, has fallen on thee.

            PEDRO.

She's gone, she's gone ! and I am all alone.

        (*Clasps her to his bosom.*)

        (*Curtain falls.*)

      END OF FOURTH ACT.

ACT V.

SCENE I.—KING'S BEDCHAMBER.

ALPHONSO *lying on a couch*—PEDRO, RUDOLPHO, *and Attendants.*

ALFONSO.

My son, before another morn shall break,
My heart shall rest, my life be passed away,
And I am fain to give thee some advice.
Be slow to act! Be caution still thy rule ;
But when thou seest a certain road to action,
Be resolute, and promptly force thy way.
Let no man know thy thoughts. Keep thy lips
    closed.
Be kingly in thy bearing to the world,
And let no kindly feeling bring it near thee ;
For if thou dost, they learn but to despise.
And is a living man more desolate
Than is a king, despised in his own realm !
Hold justice ever equal in thine hand.
Have thou no bosom friends to grieve with thee ;
For if thou dost, thy friend may speak thereof,
And make thy secret grief a laugh for all.
If thou dost pledge thyself, stick to thy pledge.

When thou shalt have thy throne, let dignity
And royal grace perch on thy golden crown,
And men will honor thee, for truth, for justice,
And for dignity.

PEDRO.

I covet not a crown, nor care I now,
How the world runs.—I'm desolate in heart.

RUDOLPHO.

Your Grace, when the leech parted from thy bed,
He said, that little speech must satisfy.

ALFONSO.

My time is short, I know it well, Rudolpho ;
And to thy care, I do commit the Prince.
Let not his anger, nor his fierce desire
For vengeance on the Queen, lead to an act
That might affront his crown, or mar his fame ;
Better to suffer wrong, than bear disgrace.
I do beseech thee, urgently, my lord,
Make my son promise, not to harm the Queen.

RUDOLPHO.

Most noble Prince, let me entreat thee now,
To hear the dying wishes of his Grace,
And to forgive the Queen, thy mother.

(*Pedro kneels beside his father, and takes his hand.*)

PEDRO.

My father, I will promise as thou askest.
I will not harm my mother anywise ;
But I do swear, holding thy royal hand,
To follow all the others to the death.
This is my oath, fixed and unchangeable.—
Justice demands that murderers be slain !

ALFONSO.

I loved thy mother once, and love her still,
And am content, thou wilt not injure her.
Pleasure thyself how thou mayest treat the rest ;
Well they deserve to bear due punishment.

PEDRO.

I will return anon, to stop, my liege—
Rudolpho, wilt thou come with me a moment ?

RUDOLPHO.

Your Grace, may I go with the Prince ?

ALFONSO.

Go with him.   [*Exeunt.*

(*Curtain falls.*)

SCENE II.—SERVANTS' HALL IN THE PALACE.

SEBASTIAN *and* MARCO.

SEBASTIAN.

'Tis just a year to-day since we left Coimbra,—
Hast heard of the Queen, Marco ?

MARCO.

Nay, nothing new ! She fled to France, when
King Alfonso died. King Pedro ordered her to leave
Portugal, and ne'er return on pain of death. She was
a bitter Queen.

SEBASTIAN.

The King doth anxious seek for Ludro, for Pechico,
and for Pauline, but they keep hid away. Would I
could find them.

MARCO.

Did not the King speak to thee o' the matter ?

SEBASTIAN.

He did, and promised me great favor. But Ludro
is quick to act, and at all times cunning as a fox.

MARCO.

Methought I saw Ludro yesterday, but it might be but fancy, and I lost him in the crowd.

Enter RODRIGO, *hastily.*

RODRIGO.

Sebastian ! Sebastian ! I have found Ludro and his hiding-place. I warrant he plays murderer no more.

SEBASTIAN.

Now be not in hot haste, or we may overshoot our mark. Marco, say not a word to any one. If it be so, we get him, it is well ; an he be not secured, no one will know our error. It may not be Ludro after all. Art sure, good Rodrigo ?

RODRIGO.

I tell thee, it is Ludro. I followed him, and I have tracked him home. Oft would he turn and look, to find if any followed. But we will watch him as a cat doth a mouse, and take him unawares. Come on, Sebastian. I swear 'tis Ludro.

[*Exeunt conversing.*

(*Curtain falls.*)

SCENE III.—PEDRO'S BEDCHAMBER.

PEDRO *and* RUDOLPHO.

PEDRO.

My good Rudolpho, it were foolishness
To search for Ludro, save in secrecy.
I'm weary now, and fain would rest myself—
Go, set the guard, and I will seek my couch.
My brain is weary, burning in my skull,
And rest and sleep will sooth my weariness;
And now, good night, my lord.

RUDOLPHO.

Good night, and pleasant rest and happy dreams!
I'll set the guards.   [*Exit.*

PEDRO.

He's gone.   Rudolpho is an honest man;
And as he went, he spoke of happy dreams!
Aye, it is true, when one doth think thereon,
That life is but a dream, a cloud, a mist,
That passeth fleetly o'er the scythe of time!
How oft in dreams, the shadow of the past,
Tingeth our fancy as with rosy tints.
Inez! and thou wert but a dream to me,—

A happy dream, thou and our loving sons.
Oh, thou didst promise with thy dying breath,
To come once more, and be my comforter.
How oft we sat together lovingly,
With thy soft cheek laid gently on my breast,
And thy fond arms encircling me in peace.
Our children played around us joyously,
And thy kind words would sooth my weariness.
Oh, I did love with more than common love,
And thou, with all a woman's lovingness.
Thy gentle spirit seems to hover nigh ;
And oft, methinks, thou gazest in my face,
And in my fancy I can hear thee breathe,
Or heave a tender sigh, as in old days.
But 'twas no dream, 'twas all reality !
Oft in the still of night, will o'er us creep
Sad musings, such as now, which do relieve
Man's weary spirit, in this weary world.

(*He retires to his couch and sleeps. Enter* INEZ,
gently leading the children. She stops before PEDRO,
*and embraces him. She points to him, and the
children come and kiss him. He moves restlessly,
and they vanish. He wakes.*)

PEDRO.

Where has she gone, and taken hence our boys ?
'Twas but a dream, but 'twas a happy dream ;

Yes, I could dream my lifetime all away,
If she returned to earth, and me, once more.

> [*Retires and sleeps.*

(*They return.* Inez *sits beside him and kisses him. The children play.*)

(*Curtain falls slowly.*)

Scene IV.—STREET IN A SEA-PORT.

Enter Pauline *and* Pechico.

Pechico.

The ship will sail at noon, so be prepared.

Pauline.

I would we were away. How I do fear
To fall into this cruel Pedro's hands.
Had I not listened to the Queen's advice,
We had been better!

Pechico.

'Tis useless now to think of this past deed.

Curse upon Ludro, but upon the Queen—
May endless curses hang above her head.
In her the wolf and viper were entwined.
Relentlessly she sought her victim's life,
Till she most fiercely seized upon her quarry.
Then in her rage, like an ungenerous hound,
Mangled the fallen prey from sheer revengefulness

Enter LUDRO.

Come, haste, my friend, the ship will quickly sail.

LUDRO.

No time to lose, Pechico, thou art right.
I must return a moment for my gold ;
Good sooth, we need it all.

[*Exit.*

(*Enter a beggar.*)

BEGGAR.

My lord and my lady, give a poor man an alms,
for poverty doth bite me to the quick.

PAULINE.

My Lord Pechico, give him an alms.

PECHICO.

Here is a piece of gold ; get bread and fill thy belly.

BEGGAR.

Heaven's blessing rest on you, I will pray for you.

[*Exit.*

PAULINE.

What keeps Ludro, and he so swift in action ?
I wish we were away from Portugal.
What doth keep Ludro ?

Re-enter beggar, in haste.

BEGGAR.

My lord and lady, fly for your lives.   The sol-
diery are abroad, and have secured one Ludro, and
they asked after thee and my lady.   See ! cast
thy coat aside, and take thou mine.

(*Shouts and noise without.*)

PECHICO.

Then give it me.   (*They exchange.*)
Now let us hence!   [*Exit* PECHICO *and* PAULINE.

BEGGAR.

He gave an alms in gold, and I repaid the gentleman as best I could, with his life.

Enter SEBASTIAN *and* RODRIGO.

RODRIGO.

My friend, sawest thou a lady and a gentleman pass by, a moment since ?

BEGGAR.

I saw many pass this way ; didst thou not meet a fat old lady and a gentleman ?

RODRIGO.

Nay, but the last thou sawest ; where went they ?

BEGGAR.

The road I saw thee come.

SEBASTIAN.

What were they like ? Tell us of them, fellow.

BEGGAR.

I told thee the lady was exceeding fat, and had white hair, the gentleman walked with a staff.

SEBASTIAN.

We have Ludro bound secure; had we Pechico and his wife, I would be most content.

RODRIGO.

It hath not been my Lord Pechico, nor Pauline. 'Tis folly to chase strangers, and be laughed at.

SEBASTIAN.

I have my doubts this beggar plays us false. I
watched his features, and methought I read a lie
in every word he spoke.

BEGGAR.

I lie not, my master; may heaven reward thee;—
give me an alms ?

RODRIGO.

I will back again, and keep mine eye on Ludro.

SEBASTIAN.

I know not what to do ; I feel my game is nigh
me. I will to the ship and watch it narrowly.

BEGGAR (*aside*).

And I will warn my friends. (*Aloud.*) For God's
sake, master, give me an alms !

SEBASTIAN.

Nay, get thee to the devil. I give not alms to
every lazy hound. Get thee to the devil, I say.

> [*Exit Beggar.*

I will make sure of Ludro when I return. Go
thou Rodrigo, keep him safely bound, and if he burst
his bonds, take thou his life. The King will be content, to get him dead or living.

> [*Exeunt different side' of stage.*

J

Scene V.—GROUNDS OF THE PALACE.

Pedro and Rudolpho.

Pedro.

Dost thou remember those last words she spoke ?

Rudolpho.

She said she would return to comfort thee.

Pedro.

Dost thou believe that there is aught in dreams ?

Rudolpho.

Night hath her fancies, as she shroudeth us ;
And when the body, weary from its labor,
Doth rest in peace, fancy wakes up again,
And acts the scenes that we had passed among.
Yet there is more than fancy in a dream ;
And few men live, who have not felt their force.
Oft in our dreams the spirits of the dead
Do show themselves to eyes within the soul ;
And spirit comes to spirit, as of yore,
And maketh our lost friendship even fresher.
Oft do I dream I see my mother's form,
Stealing around me, and with gentle voice

Telling her son, how he should guide his actions.
Dreams are realities, while they do last.

PEDRO.

They *are* realities whilst they do last!
My good Rudolpho, I did dream last night
That my lost Inez came to comfort me—
She and our children.   She sat as of yore,
Beside my bed, as we had talked together.
I saw my little ones gambling around ;—
I kissed them all, and I was full of joy!
Methought I asked about their cruel wounds,
But Inez told me that those wounds were gone,
That they were happy now in heaven.
And then a gentle peace came over me,
And that sweet dream doth comfort me e'en yet.
But look, Rudolpho !   Yonder comes a stranger.
Who is he ?   Dost thou know him ?

RUDOLPHO.

He is some wandering troubadour, who comes
To sing his song about his lady love ;
Perchance he comes to fight, or heaven knows what.

PEDRO.

Let us retire to watch how he may act;
It may be, he may sing some tale of love,
And for us 'twill be pastime.

*(They retire behind the trees. Enter a troubadour
with his guitar.)*

TROUBADOUR.

I feel so weary, I will rest myself
A little while, and sing an olden tale.　　(*Sings.*)

I.

In olden time there was a fairy land,
Where dwelt a maiden, rich and kind and fair ;
And lovers came to seek this lady's hand,
Though but for one, her heart was filled with care.

Chorus.

With a heigh-ho, heigh-ho, sing of my love,
She hath left me and gone to the blue skies above.

II.

He wooed and won her, as a courteous knight,
And pledged his troth and took his lady's hand ;
But grief came o'er them, when their hours were
　　bright,
And cast its shadow on their fairy land.

Chorus.

With a heigh-ho, heigh-ho, sing of my love,
She hath left me and gone to the blue skies above.

III.

And he was king in all her fairy land ;
A rose he planted nigh his lady's bower—

It bloomed, and was by every soft air fanned,
And two sweet rosebuds grew beside the flower.

Chorus.

With a heigh-ho, heigh-ho, sing of my love,
She hath left me and gone to the blue skies above.

IV.

Then lo ! a wicked fairy came that way,
And hatred filled her, when the bloom she saw—
She plucked the flower, and tore the buds away—
And laughed in scorn, nor heeded honor's law.

Chorus.

With a heigh-ho, heigh-ho, sing of my love,
She hath left me and gone to the blue skies above.

V.

But when the prince, alas ! had seen her slain,
And his two rosebuds trampled on the ground,
His heart was filled with rage, and grief and pain,
And time could never heal his bosom's wound.

Chorus.

With a heigh-ho, heigh-ho, sing of my love,
She hath left me and gone to the blue skies above.

VI.

He sought and slew this wicked wandering sprite,
Who killed his princess and her children dear—
But even yet his soul is dark as night,
And oft for her he drops a secret tear,

Chorus.

With a heigh-ho, heigh-ho, sing of my love,
She hath left me and gone to the blue skies above.
With a heigh-ho, heigh-ho, sing of my love,
She hath left me and gone to the blue skies above.

PEDRO *and* RUDOLPHO (*come forward*).

PEDRO.

Sir Knight, thy song is worthy of some recompense ;
So, prithee, take this gift from me.

(*Offers a purse.*)

TROUBADOUR.

I do not sing for wages, worthy sir.—
Some other time, good sooth, I'll sing thee more.

RUDOLPHO.

If thou art weary, come and rest with me,
And take refreshment.

TROUBADOUR. ♦

I'm very weary, and would rest a while ;
At least until the heat of noon be past—
And I have yet full many a league to travel.

(*Shouts without.   Much noise.*)

PEDRO.

What means this uproar ?   Are the people mad ?
Let us return my friends.   I do bethink
I see Sebastian with his weapon drawn.—
That doth betoken something !   Let us hence.
(*Shouts.*)   [*Exeunt.*

SCENE VI.—A HALL IN THE PALACE.

Enter SEBASTIAN *and* RODRIGO, *with their swords
drawn, followed by a guard with* LUDRO *in chains.*

SEBASTIAN.

When will the King be here ?

ATTENDANT.

He comes even now.

LUDRO.

Tell him to haste, that Ludro doth await him,
And I would know the mischief he doth plot.

(*Enter* PEDRO *and attendants.   He stops and looks
steadfastly at* LUDRO.   LUDRO *looks defiantly at him.*)

PEDRO.

And thou art Ludro?

LUDRO.

Yes, I am Ludro, and well thou knowest me.

PEDRO.

Prepare thee. then to die.   No mockery
Of trial shall be given thee, for guilt
Of foulest murder hangs upon thy head.
Go, bring the executioner.

> [*Exit attendant.*

(*Enter* EXECUTIONER *masked.*)

(*To executioner.*)

Seest thou that man.   Stretch him upon the rack !
Tear him from limb to limb, and sear his flesh.
See he escape thee not.   Crush every bone,
And stretch each atom of thine ingenuity,   .
To make him feel he is a murderer !
He had no pity for my wife and babes ;
When she entreated he did mock her grief,
And plunged his bloody dagger to her heart.

LUDRO.

Then know,—thy mother bid me strike the blow;
She was more fierce in her revengefulness

Than all the rest. I did but do her bidding—
Thy mother's bidding—if I murdered Inez.
Seek her, and torture her, and tear her limbs,
And sear her tender flesh, and do but justice.
I crave not pity. Thou art like thy mother.
'Twas Pauline and Pechico slew thy brats ;
They have escaped, and they can laugh at thee.
Then do thy worst on me, thou canst no more,
And even in my death, I do defy thee.

PEDRO.

(To executioner.)

In the next chamber thou wilt ply thy trade.
Sebastian, follow thou, and see the rack
Doth do its duty on mine enemy.

LUDRO.

Thou canst not shake me into craven fear—
I hate thee and thy race. Thou art a coward
And durst not strike a blow.

PEDRO.

I know thee, Ludro. Thou wouldst make me raise
My arm to slay thee, to escape the rack !
I would not foul my weapon on such carrion.

[*Exit* LUDRO, SEBASTIAN, *and executioner*,

FIRST LORD (*aside*).

He hath a spirit in him, fierce and wild,
Revenge and bitterness in all he doth.

SECOND LORD (*aside*).

He only hath his merits for his murder.

FIRST LORD (*aside*).

Yes, he doth merit all his punishment.
If luck doth bring Pechico and Pauline
Within the rigor of King Pedro's grasp,
He'll give them little grace.

PEDRO.

Let all men leave me.   I would be alone.

[*Exeunt omnes.*
(*Groans and sighs.*)

What measure can I give of punishment,
That I could pay him back his cruelty.

(*Moans and shrinks and sobs.*)

Thou hadst no mercy !—groan and sob and sigh—
I will have none on thee.   My loving wife,
Be thou revenged upon thy murderer!
But I will harrow up his living flesh,
For he hath got a mind unnatural.

(*Groans.*)

Aye, groan, and sob, and let the deathly sweat
Stream o'er thy temples, down thy livid face :
And it doth comfort me to know thou perishest !
Inez, if thou wert here, thou wouldst forgive.—
Thy tender spirit would not bear this sight.
My brain doth burn to think upon thy death.—
Thy children slain, then cast before thy face,
And those sweet noble boys, were thine and mine,—
Our pride, our joy, and all we had on earth.

(Sobs and sighs.)

Groan if thou canst—thou hadst a demon's mind,
No feeling left, but what thy carcass feels ;
Nor pity, love, nor aught compassionate,
But hate, spite, falsity, coveting all things !
Oh Inez ! Inez ! could I bring thee back,
A thousand lives like his I'd freely give.
But thou art gone, and canst return no more.

Enter SEBASTIAN.

SEBASTIAN.

Ludro is dead, my liege.

PEDRO.

Dead, sayest thou ?   Dead ?   Sebastian, is he dead ?
Hath he escaped me so ?   Go, bear him out,
And hang his carcass in the market place.
Hang it in chains, that all the world may know.—

A warning to all villains, such as he.—
My wife, my children, I have kept my oath.
Ye are revenged upon your murderer.

[*Exit, followed by* SEBASTIAN.

SCENE VII.—HALL IN THE PALACE.

MATTEO *and* RUDOLPHO.

MATTEO.

I heard of my poor sister's cruel murder,
And that the Prince hath well revenged the crime !
Ludro he hung in chains in the market place—
The Queen he banished, and all he could catch
Of those assassins that they took as guards,
He hung upon the nearest tree when caught ;
But Pauline and Pechico have escaped.

RUDOLPHO.

Was e'er such cruel murder in the earth !
Because the King did most sincerely love,
They slew thy sister Inez wantonly.
He anxiously doth seek Pechico's den,
And heaven help him and Pauline if they're taken.

Yet Pedro hath an honest, loving heart,
An he be thy friend, he shows it in each action ;
An he be thy foe, better escape in time.—
No one can wonder at his bitterness.

MATTEO.

The Prince will hearken to me if I ask,
And spare the lady's life.   As to Pechico,
Let him do as it may pleasure him.

RUDOLPHO.

I know the King full well in everything.
Beseech him not, or thou wilt raise his choler,
For he hath sworn an oath, pledging his soul
To kill them both an he can only find them.
I knew him when a boy, and know him now.—
Thou needst not waste thy breath, and do it not.

(Enter the KING *alone.)*

PEDRO.

My lords, a merry morning to you both !
My heart feels light—the sun doth pleasant shine,
And I would fain go hunting once again ;
'Twill ease the cares of all my councillors.
What say you if we take a merry week ?
A day is nothing in the summer time.

MATTEO.

As it may please your Grace, it pleaseth me—
What doth my Lord Rudolpho say of it ?

RUDOLPHO.

To wander in the wood doth ease the mind,
And is a solace and most comforting.
I do advise the King to spend a while
Roaming around, and gaining manly vigor.

PEDRO.

Then let us rise to-morrow with the dawn ;
My lord Matteo, see to horse and hound,
And thou, my good Rudolpho, come with us.
Now I bethink me, I will hunt near Spain,
And visit my old friend Count Aguilar.
Thither we'll wend our way in joyous mood,
And see those places dear to memory !
Matteo, my good friend, dost thou remember
That I was lost one evening on those hills,
Where I found one whom we have lost forever.

MATTEO.

I do remember it right well, your Grace.

PEDRO.

Then get thee hence, and get all things prepared,
The things of state must rest till we return.

(Curtain falls.)

SCENE VIII.—FOREST NEAR THE HERMIT'S CAVE.

MATTEO, PEDRO, RUDOLPHO (*standing together*).

MATTEO.

'Twas on this spot that I first saw your Grace.

PEDRO.

I well remember it.   'Twas summer time,
And not a care had I to bother me ;
Those merry days will never come again.

MATTEO.

Now let us to the cave ; 'tis close at hand.—
I fain would have a draught.   Wilt come, your
    Grace ?

PEDRO.

Aye, let us go.   We know how to return.—
I warrant that we are not lost again.

                    [*Exeunt.*

Enter SEBASTIAN *and* RODRIGO.

RODRIGO.

I saw them as they went into the cave.
He's gone to see their ancient meeting place,
And we can tell when they return again.

But who are these, coming along this way ?
Methinks I've seen them.   What sayest thou, Se-
    bastian ?

SEBASTIAN (*moving aside*).

By Heaven, I know them well ; now hide thyself—
Let us be crafty till we seize them both.
'Tis the Lady Pauline and Pechico.

RODRIGO.

See thou dost watch them closely.   I will go,
And take the King this strange and wondrous news.

SEBASTIAN.

See, there they come,—Matteo and the King.
Go warn them of the matter, and be swift.—
Make them hold back and hide.

[*Exit* RODRIGO.   SEBASTIAN *hides.*

Enter PAULINE *and* PECHICO (*cautiously*).

PAULINE.

We soon shall reach the cave to rest awhile,
For thou and I have need of rest to-night.
I'm weary of the world, and I begin
To hate it, with all hatred.

PECHICO.

Come, sit thee down. None can be watching here,
And soon we'll see the towers of Granada.

(*They seat themselves.*)

PAULINE.

Methought I heard a distant hunter's horn.

PECHICO.

And if thou didst—Cheer up, cheer up!

Re-enter RODRIGO, PEDRO, RUDOLPHO *and* MATTEO,
cautiously. PEDRO *points his finger at* PECHICO
and draws his sword. RUDOLPHO *catches his arm.*

RUDOLPHO.

(*Aside.*) Restrain thy anger but a moment.

PAULINE.

'Tis weary thus to wander through the earth,
In fear and trembling of our very shadow ;
And if we chance to fall in Pedro's hands,
We soon shall know our doom.
But thou hast been a comfort unto me,
And never once did murmur or repine.

PECHICO.

An we do safely get among the Moors,
We bid defiance to all Portugal.

K

Had I ta'en thy advice and told the Prince,
Ere we had pledged unto the cursed Queen,
The children's murder was not on our heads.

PAULINE.

I slew them not; 'twas thou.   I had no hand in't.

(PEDRO *advances a step.* RUDOLPHO *grasps his arm.*)

RUDOLPHO (*Aside*).

One moment more, my liege, a moment more !

PECHICO.

The Queen did make thee swear to murder them,
And I did murder them for thee.   But now—
Regrets mean nothing, or e'en less.

(PEDRO *and the others rush on* PECHICO *and* PAULINE.)

PEDRO.

Dost thou know me, Pechico ?   Thou sayest:
Thou hast murdered my sons.   Matteo seize on
them; Sebastian, all of you surround and make them
prisoners.   (*They do so.*)

(*Horn outside.*)

Hear ye that bugle sounding o'er the hills,
My Lord Pechico and my Lady Pauline ?
Hear it, the last day ye remain on earth !

Be quick Rodrigo, bring my huntsmen in ;—
Tell them I've caught *my* game and wait for help.

[*Exit* RODRIGO.

RUDOLPHO.

Did I not tell thee thou wouldst hear them speak,
And have not both their tongues condemned them-
    selves ?

PEDRO.

It matters not.　See, they are coming now.
Rodrigo hastens all my merry men.

(*Enter nobles and huntsmen, with bows, &c., who
    surround* PECHICO *and* PAULINE.)

My lords and gentlemen, keep them secure.
I'll punish both of them in such a mode
That all of Portugal shall blanch with fear.
They both confessed the murder of my sons,
And 'tis enough ! Sebastian, and my lords
Matteo and Rudolpho, come with me.

(*They retire.*)

FIRST LORD.

The king looks fierce, and cold, and resolute.
Didst thou observe the passion in his eye,
And how his cheeks turned pale, his lips compressed,

How every word came hissing through his teeth!
What will he do with them?

SECOND LORD.

Now seest thou him, how he doth stand alone!
His arms are tightly folded on his breast,
And sternness seems as his embodiment.
Hither he comes, his eye upon the ground,
And there is deadly mischief in his mind.

Re-enter PEDRO, *and the others.*

PEDRO.

Go, bring two stakes and plant them firmly down,
Make them secure and lead them to their doom;
Then bind until their chains will crush the flesh—
Do as I bid thee! on thy life, Sebastian!

SEBASTIAN.

Let me entreat your Grace!

PEDRO.

Nay, not one word—do as I have commanded!

RUDOLPHO.

I do beseech your Grace, do not this thing.

PEDRO.

Rudolpho, I could grant thee anything;

Didst thou not see me hold my father's hand,
And on my knee take a most solemn oath
To slay her murderers to the very last.

MATTEO.

Your Grace, I do beseech thee, let me speak!
Do not this fearful thing, I do entreat thee;
Nay, for the sake of her who was thy wife,
Who was my sister, whom we both did love;
Do not a thing which is so horrible!

PEDRO.

Seest thou yon sun, Matteo? bid him turn,
Will he once listen, when thou dost entreat?
If there was one to whom I'd give attention,
I'd give it thee—for our lost Inez' sake.
Thou knowest I have sworn a solemn oath.—
I shall not spare them, as I have a soul!
Seize on Pechico! bind him to the stake.—
Chain him so he escape me not, then bind
This woman, till her tender flesh turn black!

PECHICO.

Wreak all thy vengeance on my single head,
But spare my wife! she never did thee harm.

PEDRO.

Had she once asked to save my Inez' life,—
Had she entreated for my children's lives,

I had not punished her; she spurred thee on,
And she shall die. Guards! do your office quickly.

(*The guards bind them to their stakes.*)

Matteo, see if I have been obeyed.

MATTEO.

Your Grace, 'tis done as you commanded.

PEDRO (*to the guards*).

See ye speak not to them on pain of death;
Heed not their sighs nor moanings, groans nor sobs,
Give them no food, nor let one drop of water
Touch their lips.   (*To Pechico.*)
Remain where thou art bound, 'till thou art dead.
Behold thy wife and struggle to be free;
Let thy chains rot thy flesh from hour till hour—
Thou only canst escape when thou art dead;
Keep watch upon her that she wander not,
And when the bonds are burst, then take her down
And bury her in hell.
Inez, I've kept my vow, thou art revenged,
And our poor children's blood shall cry no more,
And thy kind spirit now may rest in peace.

[*Exit* PEDRO, *looking sternly at* PECHICO *and*
PAULINE. *The others form a half circle behind them,
the guards in their places making a tableau. Two
guards, with halberds to each prisoner.*

(*Curtain falls slowly.*)

www.ingramcontent.com/pod-product-compliance
Lightning Source LLC
Chambersburg PA
CBHW020014030726
47500CB00002B/592